REBEL WITHOUT A CREW

by Kerrie A Noor

CONTENTS

GLOSSARY

Voted Ins: Planet Hy Man's politicians. A contradiction in terms as they were never voted in. In the past, they were also known as the "Blue-Rinse Brigade," when they were young enough for hair dye to make a difference.

Whip: also known as a flesh-cracker. In the past used by Man Spies to round up men like cattle during the great coup 1958, now worn like a peacock parading its virility.

Man Spy: women bred to act like men, who captured any free men to be "cared for" and/or "appropriately employed" for the greater benefit of the planet.

Manifesto the Great: the last man to rule Planet Hy Man, he wrote his memoirs while still ruling. In fact, he was so busy writing that he didn't notice the great coup of 1958 until it was too late. His last few years were spent in exile, editing the *Hy Man's Geographic*, a magazine no one had read for years, which is now mainly used for lighting fires when the price of energy goes up. It was also he who developed the early stances of the *incognito pose*.

Incognito Pose: a pose adopted by robots and the masses, helping them to blend into the background, or at least let those of great importance know that they are not worth noticing.

Teflon: a by-product of egg popping, and a material like no other. It is so flexible that a robot made of it will never age and finds yoga as easy as the mere blink of an eye.

Telespray/Telespraying: inspired by Planet Hy Man's first truly scientific woman who had a crush on *Star Trek*'s Captain Kirk. She was an enthusiastic shower-maker who designed a power shower so strong it moved women from inside the shower to outside—she saw the potential.

For a while it was all the rage for the Voted In as they telesprayed from one shop to the next, frightening shop assistants until the shop assistants rebelled and started charging *startle* charges.

Cheese Pizza: a secret passion for many on Planet Hy Man. Once someone discovered how to make hemp pulp *sort of* taste like cheese, the pizza was revived, celebrated, and eaten whenever possible. Hemp pulp never, however, managed to work in cheese sauce.

Caffeine Blast: coffee on Planet Hy Man is for the elite and was introduced mainly to keep the Voted In awake during meetings.

Illegal Beverage: caffeine for the masses is as illegal as bootlegging was on Earth. Keeping the masses alert is greatly discouraged by those in charge; weak decaffeinated tea is all they are allowed.

Egg Popping: a recently accepted profession established by the first retired man spy. Eggs (also known as valuable real-estate) from a successful woman can earn her a tidy commission—which Mex was banking on to provide her with a better robot than the damnable Pete.

Contemplation of the Navel: a practice recognized by the robot-training board as an adequate way of making the passing of time productive, as well as cutting down on minding others' business.

Arts and Stuff: anything gift-wrapped.

Limo Drivers: the last driver retired years ago and now mans the footman's residents' reception. He never remembers any names but he does a good toasted hemp pulp.

The Scent of an Identity: women who have a "longing" or a "something is missing" feeling are more susceptible to the scent than contented women. Men are completely immune.

ESP-ing: the ability to communicate without speaking aloud; a form of mind reading. Outlawed on Planet Hy Man as it made bugging —a truly profitable pastime—pointless.

Messenger: an envelope-like device that usually contained orders of an unpopular nature.

H-Pad: looks like an iPad but has the ability to answer back and is not nearly as much fun.

Sparkly: sparkling water that tastes like champagne, costs a bomb, and can cause great clarity of thought or at least the illusion of it.

Strengtheners: like straighteners, but also work as a bugging device. For years, much was collected from what women said while straightening their hair, until it was discovered that what they talked about while grooming was pretty much the said grooming. Scientists are currently working on a handless set.

The earphone: when Manifesto the Great saw these on a Star Trek repeats he was entranced, "at last a way to block out the chatter from the other half," he exclaimed.

Mind fudging: is the only defense for mind reading. It involves not thinking about what you want to think about but rather creating a thought decoy.

Blow up & blow out: a term used for H-Pads and the like, nobody is sure of the difference except a blow-out is preferable to a blow-up.

Tablet: a homemade sweet Scots claim as their own, sort of in between fudge, and toffee but carries greater mystical qualities.

Last hoorah home: bit like a rest home but with better sandwiches.

The C-Pad, H-pad, H-pad 11 and other pad malarkey: all fore-runners of the iPad, which evolved with the *I know better than you* app some would call virus. The iPad metamorphizes from the C-Pad thanks to a liaison with Legless and very smart IT student during Legless's lost in San Francisco years.

A Scrapper: A forgotten element from a forgotten time on planet Hy Man when real animals roamed. A scrapper fed animals scraps from the food chain, it was a dirty job. Now the term is only used when pickle swearing will not do.

Hilda's energy plan: Similar to Beryl's but with more options.

Balancing platform: Hilda dreamed of a balancing platform from the day she was first ask to go out and pick herbs in the compound. She looked at the muddy field and thought there must be a better way.

Jock strap: One of man's best kept secrets on Planet Hy Man. All men on Planet Hy Man looked well-endowed and woman never knew why.

Alice: similar to Amazon's Alexa's with many of *the I know better than you* bugs still intact. No metamorphizes or IT students involved.

MEET THE GANG-PLANET HY MAN

Legless: a man from Planet Hy Man who is past his prime. No one knows why he is called Legless, but he is a man elusive as a shadow, as well as the reason for the whole saga that you are about to read.

Beryl: a woman way past her prime. She is the leader of Planet Hy Man and has been since this whole saga began—and intends to remain so.

Mex: a woman from Planet Hy Man who is as angry as she is courageous. She is of the age where a pension is within her grasp and smart enough to be planning for it.

Woody: a dwarf from Earth, unemployed but young enough to still have hope.

Vegas: a young ambitious woman from Planet Hy Man. She believes in many things but is logical enough to know when to ditch said beliefs.

Hilda: a woman from Planet Hy Man who has more ambition in her little finger than an American running for president. She is in her prime and will step on anyone who dares argue.

Pete: Mex's robot—or android, as he likes to call it. Pete has plans and is smart enough to keep them well hidden.

Don: a cabbie from Glasgow with a soft spot for the character below . . .

Bunnie: a round woman who puts one in mind of Dawn French. She has a way with men, dogs, and lonely women. Except in times of stress, when she throws such "ways" to the wind for a more dominating/shouting approach.

DJ: a young DJ born in Glasgow. He is the same age as Woody and as tall as Woody is short. He is a man frustrated with his mentor, who is also the character below . . .

Archie: an Earthly pensioner who is old enough to know better and old enough not to care. His advice is ignored by many.

DBO: a teenager from Planet Hy Man. She is ignored by many, and she would like to change the status quo but is not sure how.

H2: a twenty-year-old woman from Planet Hy Man. She looks and acts much older than her years, which is probably the reason no one hangs around her.

Baby: one of the youngest of the Voted In who was actually voted in by the Voted In. It was either that or put up with her constant complaints on the radio where she worked before becoming a Voted in.

Senator: a rare Voted In with a conscious, she had the same privileged background as Beryl. She was one of the first to have no father; her mother did have some feeling for those lower than her and was often seen buying things in the market to boost the economy.

Pot, Prudence and Pope: the other three Robot 33. Like Pete they are smart but unlike Pete not smart enough to hide it.

Verruca: Is H2's gran a savvy woman who deserves a better name.

Eunice and Patsy: Bunnies' neighbours. A couple who firmly believes that a couple who argue together stay together, their making up is legendary.

New additions

Alterationist: Women of hippy origin who can make anything from anything; recycling to them is second nature and what they can do with a potato sack is nothing short of a miracle.

PREVIOUSLY ON PLANET HY MAN

The gang have made it to the Edinburgh Festival and are camping in a caravan park.

They traced Legless to the Lizard Lounge along with a couple of drag queens plugging their own show. Mex discovers vodka, while H2 discovers her greatest pal DBO is still alive and not only kicking but working on a new plan.

Legless has proved to be a disappointment. He and Beryl had a dust-up, which has Beryl in a sea of guilt and Legless craving revenge.

Patsy has discovered the box with the wiry thing—a spare part from the plugulator, absolutely necessary for telespraying back to Planet Hy Man. The question is, will she discover what it's for and connect with Planet Hy Man?

Hilda, having miscalculated the shed explosion, attempted to put it out with water, leading to her flying across the yard like a stunned and plucked chicken.

DBO has escaped to the Black Hills in search of Vegas. Her plan is merely to save her planet, recruiting Vegas en route.

PROLOGUE

*H*ilda woke up to a tentative knock on her door and a throbbing head. She didn't answer but rubbed her hand across a large bump on her forehead.

It felt as large as the Black Hills.

There was another knock . . .

"Ma'am?"

"What is it?"

"I have a parcel."

"Just slip it through the slitty thing . . ."

"It's not the slip-able kind."

"Well then, just leave it outside the door."

"It's not leave-able either."

Hilda tutted.

"It is but take-able," added the robotic voice.

"Take-able? What are you talking about?" said Hilda as she rubbed her bump. *You could ride a floating platform around it,* she thought.

"It says here," the voice read, "it is to be *hand*-delivered into our esteemed leader's hands only. Definitely *not* leave-able."

Hilda, with a great muttering of "pickles," staggered out of bed. She caught a glimpse of her face in the mirror and almost staggered again—it would be days before she could leave the pad with this face. She'd be laughed out of the room with a view before she even opened her mouth.

"Turn the other way," snapped Hilda.

"What?"

"When I open the door, you must turn the other way, or I won't open the door."

"Turning as we speak, ma'am."

Hilda creaked the door open a few inches and peered into the blinking eyes of a delivery android.

"Great pickled egg," said the android.

"I told you to turn away."

"You took me by surprise," said the android.

"You are a robot, you don't do surprise."

"A figure of speech, ma'am. And it's *android*."

Hilda stared at the so-called android. *When did they get so smart?*

She snatched the parcel and made to slam the door, but the android stopped it with her foot.

"Signature, ma'am."

"What?"

"New rules. Signing required for parcels larger than an H-Pad or Alice is involved."

Hilda wrenched the door open, giving the android, along with her footman, a complete view of the esteemed leader in a onesie the size of a marquee, hair like a toilet brush, face as puffy as a blowfish, and a larger-than-life thumping red lump pulsating on her forehead.

"You could ride a floating platform around that bump," muttered the footman.

Hilda threw him a look, grabbed the cheap-as-a-pickle signature pad, scribbled an esteemed-leader signature, and thrust it back into the android's hands.

"You have both seen nothing."

"Memory banks wiped, ma'am," said the android.

"My lips are sealed, ma'am," said the footman.

"Just as well," said Hilda and, with a *you dare tell anyone* look, slammed her door shut.

Hilda tossed the parcel onto the chair and missed. It clattered to the ground. She stared at a mirror and touched her bump. She looked like a back of a robotic turtle.

She listened to the android reversing.

"Hemp oil won't even touch that," muttered the footman.

"Should have used filtered ice," said the android.

"Too late now," muttered the footman. "It'll be days before that thing vanishes."

"I can hear," snapped Hilda, then stopped. *Did that parcel just move?*

Grrrrrrrr . . .

She poked it with her foot.

Grrrrrrrr . . .

The parcel began to vibrate.

She nudged it again with her foot.

The vibrations grew stronger, propelling it across the floor . . .

What the pickle?

Verruca, clutching an old-fashioned but still-fit-for-purpose remote, stared at a set of plans on her equally old and fit-for-purpose kitchen table.

She sipped her hot weak tea.

The plans were one of many that she had "pilfered" years ago during the great digital take-over when paper plans were burned on large bonfires.

It had been rolled up for years; to keep it flat, she had placed a teapot on one corner and a biscuit tin on the other.

She stared down at the layout of Hilda's penthouse. Luckily, Hilda was not the redecorating sort of leader.

"It's working," said Verruca. "There may only be a forward and back on this so-called remote, but it's working—I can move the parcel."

Her robot, clattering about the inside of her fridge, didn't answer.

The screen on top of the fridge wobbled.

"Will you leave the fridge," said Verruca.

Her robot slammed the fridge door shut and the screen toppled onto its side.

"Leave where?" said the robot, adjusting the screen upright.

"Leave it where it is but *shut*," said Verruca.

"Shutting completed."

"Good, now go and do something useful," said Verruca.

"Clean fridge." The robot opened the fridge.

"No, I can't see the screen when you open the fridge . . ."

The screen wobbled.

Verruca sighed.

"No screen in fridge," said the robot.

"The screen is on top, and if you keep opening and shutting—"

"Shut door," said the robot with a robust slam.

The screen crashed to the floor.

Hilda stared at the parcel. The vibrating stopped, she waited . . . nothing.

She decided to go back to bed and, in the vain hope that the footman was wrong, slapped hemp oil on her face.

Maybe, when she woke, her face would return to normal.

Chapter One

DBO

"A good footman always knows who to spread a secret to." – Beryl

*D*BO stood at the same "no need to shut" gate Vegas had stood at.

She inhaled the damp air. She knew the moment the shed exploded that there was no turning back. And did she care?

Not one jot.

She felt excited, liberated, a new woman. All her life she had been waiting for something *big* to happen, something better than, well, anything so far, and here she was—out into the unknown, advising Vegas, the biggest Voted In since Hilda herself.

She stopped for a moment to take it all in . . .

This was her chance to make her mark, change things, and the thought thrilled her.

"I am going in," she said to Verruca. "When there is saving to be done, you can't hang around."

"And Vegas," said Verruca. "She knows you're coming?"

"Vegas is in panic mode—I think Hilda may have made contact," said DBO.

Verruca chuckled. "Don't you worry about Hilda, I have her in hand."

Vegas waited for the so-called fairy godmother on the veranda. Squinting into the distance, she wondered how she was making it through the fields. She hadn't heard a pickling word for ages.

What was taking her so long?

Unlike Vegas, DBO's curiosity gave her no time for fear. She was making her way through the fields like a scientist, taking notes. To her, the fields were a thing of fascination. She had, like many, heard little of what was outside the city and, like a few, often wondered what it was like. She had asked many times, but no one seemed to know apart from Verruca, whose only comment was "All in good time."

She moved across the stony footpath like an expert walker, her tough shoes impervious to the dry stones and odd mud patch. Her clothes, hard and scratchy, were similar to the workers' and gave her protection against the rain and wind. In fact, the fieldworkers assumed she was one of them, lost from another field. She had the walk of a worker, she took notes like a worker, and she didn't wave, even when the odd head appeared from the high hemp crops. Workers never waved; they had been brought up to be invisible.

DBO carried on, her imagination in full flow as her face was pelted by the rain, followed by a biting wind, then a scorching sun. It was a continual cycle of hot and cold that had her pondering how anyone could work in such conditions—conditions that made the shed seem like a palace.

"Which field you heading?" shouted one of the workers.

DBO looked up. She saw three weather-beaten faces peering from the high hemp grass.

"Or are you lost?" said another.

DBO stopped. "You talking to me?"

"Don't see anyone else on the road," said a worker.

DBO stopped and smiled. "Well, that is true."

Vegas looked at the sun making its way down toward the horizon. *How long did it take to walk through the fields?*

"She'll be there a while," muttered Prudence. "Those workers are a curious lot; seeing nothing but hemp can do that to a woman."

"Women? Those workers are women?" said Vegas.

"Of course, what did you think they were?"

"Well, workers . . . never really thought about them being all feeling, all moaning women . . . like, well, *me*." Vegas eyed Prudence. "You sure? I mean aren't they another more, you know, robotic sort of thing?"

"No, just women," muttered Prudence.

Vegas squinted into the horizon. "I couldn't even last an hour in that field. How do they stand it?"

"They don't," said Prudence. "They usually squat."

DBO stood at the edge of the field as three workers made their way onto the road. They eyed each other as the wind died down.

Up close, DBO looked nothing like a fieldworker. Her skin was white and smooth, a sight new to the fieldworkers. Worker One reached out to touch her pale cheek; the rough skin of her forefinger scratched against DBO's cheek, but DBO didn't flinch. Instead, she touched the face of the worker and felt the leathery face.

DBO had seen brown wrinkled skin on women at the market stalls, but these women were blacker, muscular, and much taller. Worker One's gnarled finger moved to DBO's hair as Worker Two blurted out questions.

Soon, DBO was explaining like an animated storyteller the life of a shed Operator as the sun came out (yet again) and began to burn her skin.

"You work inside?" said Worker One.

"Yes." DBO squinted at her.

"In a shed?"

"She said that already," said Worker Two. "The shed is for communicating?"

"We put tools in ours," said Worker One.

"We did have tools, but not anymore," said DBO.

"Yeah, that'll be right," said Worker Two. "A worker with no tools." She pulled a face. "A worker ain't a worker without tools." She turned to Worker Three. "Ain't that right?"

Worker Three didn't answer. She, pondering such curious ways of using a shed, was scribbling notes.

"Too right," said Worker One.

DBO talked of her footman (leaving out the massages) and how she recycled old equipment to intercept the enemy (bragging just a little) and finally ended with, as she called it, "the phantasmagorical explosion of the shed" with an illustrative *capow!*

The fieldworkers looked unimpressed.

"Our tools are incombustible."

"Really?" said DBO, breaking out in a sweat.

"Need to be, you should try working with hemp effluent under this sun."

DBO, who had never heard of hemp effluent, was about to ask what it was when Worker One began a barrage of questions on why she was here and where she was going.

DBO, trying to keep Verruca's plan *hush-hush*, talked of Earth, Beryl's landing, and a dwarf named Woody, who "once seen could never be forgotten."

The fieldworkers' eyes widened. Even Worker Three stopped writing, pencil hovering. "A dwarf?" she said. "That's the stuff of legends."

"And Beryl is our leader?" said Worker One. She turned to Worker Two. "We have a leader, is that the stuff of legends?"

"You have more than one," said DBO.

"More than one? That's taking it too far," said Worker One.

"Ridiculous," muttered Worker Three.

"Hilda," said DBO.

"Beryl *and* Hilda," scribbled Worker Three.

DBO began to describe the Voted In and the much-talked-about *room with a view.*

The three fieldworkers looked from one to the other and started to laugh.

"And this woman with those stupid gloves for shoes, she is one of those?" said Worker Three.

"Well, yes?" said DBO. "Apparently the room with a view is so high that we women below look like ants."

Worker Three began to scribble. ". . . look like ants . . ."

"Well, they know nothing about walking, I can tell you. Her shoes were as ridiculous as two leaders."

The three workers chuckled.

"Those shoes were as good at being shoes as I am a man," said Worker One.

Worker Two let forth a roar of laughter, startling Worker Three from her writing.

DBO didn't see the joke.

"You don't like puns?" said Worker Two.

"Puns?" muttered DBO.

Worker Two let out a louder roar which echoed across the field. A sea of heads popped up. DBO started to count and stopped at twenty.

Chapter Two

VERRUCA

"Pickles is for swearing, not for eating." –Cook

Hilda looked at her reflection. The hemp oil had no effect on her puffy face. In fact, if anything, she looked worse; the whole side of her face was now like a balloon. She could hardly move her lips.

So much for a good night's sleep.

Hilda dimmed the lights and wrapped a head scarf around her face, *like a good old-fashion Earth terrorist.*

She turned to Alice. "Switch on spy mode."

"Ma'am," said Alice.

"Let's start with the kitchen," said Hilda through swollen lips.

Alice projected an image of the kitchen onto a blank wall. Hilda poured herself some sparkly, pulled a straw from a drawer, and watched . . .

The dark lady who considered herself the head cook was casually leaning on her bench, eyeing Lilia. Lilia was on pot-scrubbing duty, and the dark lady was instructing Lilia like she had never cleaned one before. Lilia, attacking the bottom of a pot with a wire brush, hummed to herself. She'd had a great morning, and nothing the dark lady said could dull her mood.

"The Voted In are loving the cycling," said Lilia.

The dark lady tutted. "You're cleaning it all wrong."

Lilia, with a hum, brushed hair from her eyes. "I made scones for them," she said.

Hilda jolted in her chair. *Scones?* she thought. *Since when are scones appropriate in the basement?*

"Yes, they love them," said Lilia. "Gobbled them up—no complaints."

The dark lady choked on her tea. "They gobbled up your scones?"

"They even paid extra for hemp butter," said Lilia.

"Pay?" yelled Hilda.

The two cooks stopped. Where did that voice come from?

Hilda threw a look at Alice. "Use the silencer," she mouthed.

"Ma'am," said Alice, "the silencer has been affected by the shed explosion."

"Great pickling egg," shouted Hilda.

The two cooks stopped.

"We are on spy lock-down," said Alice.

"Spy lock-down! How can I spy when there is a pickling lock-down?"

The two cooks looked at each other.

"Who's that?" hissed Lilia.

The dark lady looked about the kitchen. There was no one, not even a mechanical mouse.

Hilda waved a "switch it off" to Alice . . .

Alice tried to explain that switching off was not an instant thing. "Spy lock-down," she said, "caused stalling . . . it will take time, ma'am."

"Time," snapped Hilda. "I have no time for *time*. Switch to the cleaners."

"Cleaners?" muttered the dark lady.

Lilia looked at the dark lady. "Thought that was me."

Hilda nodded a "switch quickly" look at Alice.

There was a rustling of noise as channels were changed; a loud piercing squeal filtered into the kitchen and Hilda's bedroom. Hilda cupped her ears as the dark lady swore, while Lilia carried on cleaning.

"That'll be the spy lock-down," said Lilia over a loud scraping.

"And that'll be you through to the other end if you keep that up," snapped the dark lady.

Hilda focused on her wall as an image of Cleaner One and Cleaner Two slowly appeared. They were casually standing outside the barracks, talking about the Voted In's lack of gratitude.

"That's the seaside resort up and running, and do they care? Are they interested?" said Cleaner One.

"No appreciation," muttered Cleaner Two.

"'Rather have a hoover robot suck my nose,' said one of 'em."

"As if they know what a hoover is," said Cleaner Two.

"'Teeth clamped together and eat through a straw,' said that so-called Baby," snapped Cleaner One.

"Bit rich. Many would give their eyeteeth for a turn of the seaside. I know I would," said Cleaner Two.

Cleaner One eyed her colleague. "Eyeteeth? Since when does a cleaner have any of those?"

"Well, if I had one, I would . . . gladly . . ."

Hilda sighed. "Is this what I pay these workers for?" she snapped. "To stand around idly chatting—"

Cleaner One stopped. "What was that?"

"Sounded like Hilda," said Cleaner Two.

"Hilda?" said Cleaner One. "She's unavailable, some say on holiday."

"Holiday?" said Cleaner Two. "She's as likely to take one of those as a Voted In is to say thank-you."

"I heard her face is like hemp pulp," said Cleaner One.

Hilda glanced at herself in a mirror. *Hemp pulp?*

"Or was it mashed pumpkin?"

"Hmmm," said Cleaner Two. "Too late for hemp oil . . ."

Hilda, with a sigh, told Alice to switch off. Spying was pointless with the lock-down in progress. She huffed; she hadn't banked on the Voted In liking the stationaries or designing bras from G strings. She thought they'd be begging for their *room with a view* back, working hard for brownie points.

"Just tell me one thing," said Hilda to Alice. "How do they pay?"

"It is more *bribe* rather than *pay*, ma'am."

"Impressive," muttered Hilda. "Never thought they had it in them." She moved to her patio doors and glanced out onto her minions below.

"Yes, ma'am. The control of the kitchen appliance is all in the peddle power of the Voted In, which they have used to their advantage —so to speak."

"Hmmm," muttered Hilda. She was bored. She couldn't spy, couldn't go out, couldn't even sip her beverages without a straw.

Grrrrrrr. The parcel moved.

She looked at it. She usually loved parcels, ripped them open in seconds even when she knew what was inside. But not this time; she had no idea what was inside or how it moved, and she couldn't care less. She had as much interest in that parcel as she did in a footman.

What had happened to her? Was it the explosion? The bump?

"Would you like to open the parcel, Alice?" she said with a flat sigh.

Alice circled the room with excitement as her arms unfolded. "Certainly, ma'am."

Everyone hated Alice, even Hilda. She was, thanks to a dysfunctional app, too eager to please, too grateful for attention, and always looking for a "well done."

Now, thanks to Hilda's face looking like the top of a pumpkin, Alice was the only robot she wanted. In fact, she found Alice's gratitude reassuring in the midst of not knowing what to do and feeling like a fool. Alice circling the penthouse with a hemp duster while offering "hot drinks" cheered her. Besides, no one listened to Alice; even if she shouted from the Speech Balcony that "Hilda's face was like a splattered hemp rissole," no one would listen. Her face was safe in the hands of Alice.

Hilda turned back to her patio doors as Alice attacked the parcel with relish. A bird fluttered by, took one look at Hilda's face, and crashed into the glass with a shriek.

Hilda, tight-lipped, pulled the curtains shut as Alice pulled what looked like a drill from the box and squealed with girlish glee.

A leaflet fluttered to the floor.

Hilda started, turned, and for a moment felt a small pulse of *interest*.

"Such decoration," muttered Alice. She turned it in her hand. "And so flexible, and yet . . . firm."

"All that work for something to screw things?" muttered Hilda.

"Ma'am," said Alice, "it is not a drill."

Hilda, with a "what is it then" on the tip of her tongue, spied the leaflet.

Hilda looked down at the instructions. She'd never see diagrams like this before, not with a woman smiling. She began to read. Soon she had forgotten all about her puffy face and her disguise as Alice discreetly left the room.

Verruca was outside preparing a bonfire when her robot, in siren mode, began to yell, "Warning, warning, map moving, map moving."

Verruca glanced at the kitchen window to see her robot circling the table, arms flying, in complete panic mode—an unattractive quality of earlier models.

Verruca raced inside.

"I told you before, it is merely the wind moving the map."

She stared at the map spread out on the table. It was moving around the table in a circular movement, with the area marked "Hilda's Bedroom" lit up like a hot plate.

Hilda had taken the bait.

She messaged DBO. "Time has been bought. Use it well."

Chapter Three

VEGAS

"Dictatorship suits you." —Letters to Hilda (writer unknown)

Vegas saw DBO's tiny figure in the distance. She had waited all night for this so-called fairy godmother. She had watched the sun go down and come up again only to find the person who was going to save everything was a shed worker, an Operator. She watched the slip of a girl walk fearlessly through the scarecrows, ignoring the birds. Vegas had no memory of her. Who noticed a shed worker? They all looked the same.

She waved.

DBO, aware of the danger of waving close to mechanical birds, nodded.

A parrot fluttered across to Vegas and nestled on her shoulder. She waved it away. It squawked into her ear; she cursed and tried a futile dodge and stepping-away motion. The bird fluttered in the air and flew back on her shoulder just as DBO strode onto the veranda.

"Where have you been?" snapped Vegas.

"Investigating, gathering information, taking it all in," said DBO. "The fieldworkers have a lot to say."

"Fieldworkers?" said Vegas.

DBO nodded.

Another, larger parrot flapped onto Vegas's head as it struggled to gain balance. Vegas swore, flapped at it, and, when it pecked, swore again.

Vegas rubbed her hand. "The birds don't bother you?"

"It's all in the body language," said DBO. "So the fieldworkers tell me."

The parrot nestled into Vegas's hair; a few strands tumbled to the floor. Vegas attempted another "get away" wave.

"Especially the waving," said DBO.

Vegas stopped mid wave.

"The birds respond to a more dismissive approach," said DBO, sending an approaching parrot squawking in the other direction.

Vegas eyed DBO. She had expected a woman like herself—hesitant, apprehensive, and, well . . . older, a woman who would enjoy and, yes, need a guided tour. In fact, she had planned one, with quirky asides and puns. DBO looked about as interested in a guided tour as Hilda in abstract art. This young slip of a thing was unmoved, steely, and, quite frankly, off-putting.

Vegas fumbled with her words.

"Well then, let's get down to the escorting."

"Escorting?" said DBO.

"Yes," she said. "And get away from these pickling birds for a start."

DBO said nothing.

"Nobody should go through this place alone," continued Vegas.

DBO looked around at the patio and pulled out a notebook.

"Well, at least for the first time," said Vegas.

Silence . . .

"We could start with the greenhouse, the robots are dying to meet you . . . the smell is bad, gets worse, and then . . . well . . ." Vegas feigned a chuckle. "It gets better . . ." She faltered. "And there are noises, weird noises, but don't mind, just leaves rustling—the odd mouse . . ." She tried a smile. "So those pesky robots say."

Vegas stopped. DBO was nosing around the veranda, taking notes, like an inspector—ignoring *her*.

She tried to explain about the three robots and was just going through their names when she caught DBO's blank face.

Was she listening?

"You'll need to mind how you go," snapped Vegas. "Let me do the talking."

DBO peered at a plant and scribbled on her pad.

"It's one thing watching these things on a screen," said Vegas, "quite another to be in the *thick of it*, so to speak."

DBO looked up from her notepad. "In the *thick of it?*"

"Yes, it is said a lot around here, along with *bee's knees*."

"Bee's knees?" said DBO, making for the door.

Vegas, attempting to stop DBO, skidded on a pile of leaves.

DBO righted her.

Vegas, with a tetchy huff, brushed herself down. "Look, smart bum—you may have just skipped through the Black Hills, scared off a few birds, made best pals with the fieldworkers, but I am still the Voted In around here and you the shed worker."

"That you have never heard of," said DBO.

Vegas stopped. "Well yes."

"Who you don't recognize?"

Vegas blushed.

"Who saved your bum?" said DBO. She made to knock at the door again, but Vegas grabbed her arm.

"Nothing can prepare you for this place," said Vegas.

DBO gestured to the door. "It says 'Enter'."

"I am just trying to say, nothing is what it seems here," said Vegas.

"Like home then?" said DBO.

"There's fish for a start," muttered Vegas.

"So I heard."

"And crazy noises," said Vegas.

DBO, looking unconvinced, gestured to the door. "So, what's in there that I should be so afraid of?"

"Women, some dressed as men—even acting like them."

"Bit like yourself then," said DBO.

"Well, yes, if you call silk . . . manly," said Vegas.

DBO sat down and rubbed her feet. "What I wouldn't give for a foot rub. That dust is a killer on the feet ."

"Tell me about it," muttered Vegas.

DBO sighed. "My footman can rub a foot, I can tell you. I couldn't get enough."

Vegas almost smiled. "I know the feeling."

"You do?" said DBO. Her face softened.

"Need to give you a shot of my drill," said Vegas. "Sorry, it's not a drill. At first I thought it was, but, well, it's not . . . can't remember what the robots called it."

"The robots—what would they know about drilling?" said DBO.

Vegas stopped her.

"If you think a foot massage is something, wait till you try my . . . um . . . drill."

"A drill by any other name still drills," said DBO.

"And"—Vegas pulled DBO closer to her—"it doesn't go near the foot."

"Where does it go?" said DBO.

"And it doesn't require a footman," whispered Vegas.

"Oh," said DBO, disappointed.

Chapter Four

THE DORMITORY

"Every woman and her robot knew what to do apart from the leader." —Manifesto the Great's Wife's Diary

The Operators stood in the kitchen of their dormitory staring at the dismantled H-Pad II. Operator One licked her fingers and nudged it; the H-Pad II rattled like a broken clock.

They were tucking into scones and hot coffee. As the scones had been liberally spread with the hemp butter and soya cream, some were feeling a touch squeamish; but, as they had no idea what to do next apart from eat more scones, they continued to tuck in, letting forth the odd belch. They were still trying to absorb the sight of Hilda losing it. Watching a dominant, intimidating bully uselessly toss water like a robot with its *let's be logical* app missing can do that to an Operator, especially when everyone else (including the half-witted kitchen footman) knew it was the equivalent of throwing oil on a flame.

The explosion of the shed had the Operators questioning everything, including: Why should such idiots as Hilda and the Voted In have the best of everything while they, the Operators who made running the planet possible, did it all on weak tea and no air conditioning?

Their leader was nothing more than, well, a woman with a body that broke like everyone else's. Who, in the face of possible danger, acted like a mechanical mouse with a screw loose.

Why should they knock their pan out for her, or for that matter, for anyone?

After the shed explosion, the Operators silently watched as the cleaners guided a speechless Hilda to the kitchen to "see to her needs." Then, when the chief called for Alice to come and "take care of things," they escaped. The last thing they wanted was to see Alice circling the area, making useless comments, and causing chaos under the name of tidying up. Alice was as good at tidying up as she was at closing a drop-down screen.

With a sack load of scones (nobody was watching) and a *keep this to yourself* look from the cook, they headed for their dormitories. Decisions were best made with coffee, scones, and butter, so they told themselves. The truth was, they had no idea what to do, and a day later, they still had no idea and had only made their way through half of the scones.

Hilda was, according to a footman, out of action for the foreseeable future. Apparently, someone had seen her face and described it as a cross between scrambled tofu and a rissole dropped from the speech balcony.

"She tried hiding her face behind a scarf," said one footman.

"The good old-fashioned Earth terrorist look," muttered the secretary with a mouth full of scone.

The Operators looked at her. "What would you know about a terrorist?"

"Enough to know that *that* disguise works as well as a mechanical parrot disguised as a homing pigeon."

"She has a point," muttered the voice from the back.

No one argued. The blasting of mechanical parrots was the male's last triumph during the Great War of the sexes and almost swung things in their favor. Women passed data via mechanical parrots disguised as homing pigeons (due to a so called mix-up of breeds), and for a while, fields were littered with the debris of blasted mechanical parrots.

"Of course, the spy lock-down doesn't help," continued the secretary. "In fact, it's probably the reason that she is now incognito."

"How do you know that?" said Operator Two.

"The whole system is as buggered as a blasted mechanical parrot. I mean how can you spy when the mute system is debunked? Everyone knows that's the first to go and the hardest to sort."

For the first time ever, the Operators looked at each other each thinking the same thing. Keeping the lock-down locked down could be the beginning of something. A something they weren't sure they wanted or could succeed in doing.

Operator Three looked down at the H-Pad 11. "We have decapitated it," she said.

They looked from one to the other.

"Only we knew how to do that," said Operator Three.

"Exactly," said the voice from the back.

"So . . ." said the Operator One.

Operator Three ushered the footman out of the dormitories and shut the door. She looked from one to the other. "Are you thinking what I'm thinking?"

Operator Four belched. "That cream was a step too far?"

"No," snapped Operator Two. "Who is going to run things?" she hissed.

"I knew that," said Operator Four. "Just joking, lightening the mood. It's all been a bit heavy around here, can't think without someone somewhere getting all dramatic."

"You can't think, full stop," said Operator One.

"Don't you *full stop* me—where would you be without me?" said Operator Four.

"The curtains in the room with a view would still work for a start," muttered the secretary.

Operator Four huffed, slapped extra cream on her scone, and, with a glare, shoved the whole lot into her mouth. Cream oozed from the side of her mouth.

"Shhhh," hissed Operator Three. "I hear a footman coming."

"Now there's a joke," mumbled Operator Four with a spray of cream.

The footman knocked on the open kitchen door. "Err, ma'am? Is this what we call you now?"

The Operators looked at each other.

"We're all the same," said the secretary, who had communist notions.

"But feel free," said Operator One, putting on her posh voice, "to *ma'am* when you see fit."

"Ma'am," said the footman. "The cleaner robot is here."

Operator One opened the door an inch and peered through the crack. "We're okay at the moment—we can wash up ourselves."

"It's not about the washing," shouted the cleaner robot. "The cook sent me."

"The cook sent her here?" mouthed Operator Two. "We're busy," she shouted.

"Yes," shouted the secretary.

"Ma'am, the cook said her job is to man the kitchen *only*," said the footman.

"So?" said the Operators in unison.

"Well, there's more manning than the kitchen, and as you are now situated in the room with a view, you are, so to speak, to earn your truckload of scones."

Operator Four coughed on her scone.

The cleaner robot arrived, tugging Hilda's floating pad behind her. "Found floating about the Building of Opulence," she said. "Parking bay required."

"We got a spare bedroom," muttered the secretary.

Operator Two nudged her and hissed, "Don't mention the spare rooms."

"And this," said the cleaning robot, placing a set of deluxe headphones on the bench. "They were found in the room with a view."

Operator One turned the earphones in her hand . . . they were sleek, built for comfort, and light, a model they had never seen before. The Operators passed it around with interest until the footman interrupted them. "Oh, and ma'am, the cook is refusing to go to the market."

"What?" said Operator Two.

"Due to overtime."

"Overtime?"

"Yes, apparently taking care of a sick leader cut into their day. The cupboards, so to speak, are empty, and as they don't get paid for working overtime, they are refusing to fill said cupboards."

Chapter Five

THE CHIEF AND THE ASSISTANT

"There's more to saving this planet than making friends with every worker you pass." —Pope

BO followed Vegas . . .

Vegas decided to make a detour to the kitchen and, hopefully, the library, where the drills were kept.

The chef, rolling pastry, was in full flow; the library was having a stock check and she was the last to know. She talked of misplaced recipe books and their so-called new system as her assistant, trying to trap a zigzagging mechanical mouse with a jam jar, swore with every pickle she could think of.

"I mean what's wrong with the old faithful Dewey system?" said the chef. "Good enough for those Earth morons . . ."

"Come here, you great pickling curd!" shouted the assistant.

The chef told her there were visitors and chores, but the assistant didn't hear . . .

The mouse shot past the apprentice, almost daring her to kick, which she did, in a temper, skidding onto her backside. The mouse disappeared under a cupboard with just his tail wagging mockingly at the apprentice.

"Why you dirty little—"

"Leave it," muttered the chef.

The apprentice, ignoring the "leave it," scrambled for the tail. It slipped through her fingers and made for the open pantry.

"Come here you . . . rodent!" She slammed the pantry shut. The cleaning rota, a good old-fashioned write-on-and-wipe-off board, crashed to the ground.

The chef caught Vegas's eye and tutted. "She's been trying to catch that thing for weeks."

The apprentice caught sight of her audience mid bend. "And you just watch like it is one of those Earth sitcoms."

"You're much funnier," said the chef.

The mouse dashed from the pantry to the fridge and disappeared.

"If you're going to catch something," said the chef, "best wait till it thinks it's safe."

The apprentice rolled her eyes.

The chef, with a sniff, slid her hand under the fridge and retrieved the mouse via its tail.

"It's not real, is it?" muttered DBO.

Vegas hushed her.

The chef, holding the mouse by its tail, inspected it like it was the first she had ever seen.

"Gran says robotic animals are best left to themselves."

"Gran?" said the chef.

"Verruca."

"Oh, her?" muttered the chef.

"She says caring for mechanical animals is not what they're made for."

The chef, with a soft face, said, "Some miss caring and patting."

"I pickling don't," snapped the apprentice. Attempting to reattach the board, she stood back, and as it crashed to the ground again, she muttered, "Bollocking pickle."

"Yes, but it's mechanical . . ."said DBO.

Vegas threw her a "shut it" look.

DBO, ignoring Vegas, continued, "You just need to pull—"

"The key?" said the chef, pulling one from the butt of the mouse. With a squeak, it flopped like a rag doll.

"Well, yes," said DBO.

The chef tossed the mouse at the bin in the corner. It bounced from one wall to the other before landing squarely in the bin.

"Shot!" The chef laughed.

The assistant, mid attaching of the board, watched with a "here we go" look.

The chef looked at DBO with interest. "You're on the ball. What's your name, luv?"

DBO told her name and was about to expand about *her* exploding shed, hopefully with her now-well-rehearsed *capow!* ending, when Vegas nudged her to "shut it" *yet again*.

DBO threw her another "I think I know when to shut it" look.

The board again tumbled to the ground, and the assistant sighed.

"No one bothers with the rota," she muttered. "I mean it's me and me that does the cleaning around here."

No one heard her.

"Who needs a rota?" she muttered to herself, ramming the board on top of the mouse in the bin.

Squeak!

The chef turned to DBO. "If you're looking for the library . . ."

"Library?" said DBO.

"Where the drills are kept," whispered Vegas.

"Then you'll need to wait," said the chef. "There's stock-taking in progress."

With the library shut, Vegas led DBO to the greenhouse.

DBO thought of Verruca and the footman. They weren't like all the others, talking over her like she wasn't there; they believed in her, believed that she could turn things around and save the planet.

"Verruca has given me a map," she said.

Silence . . .

"She knows everything, she said they have found a whole new way of eating here."

"Really?" said Vegas, half listening.

"She says that whole hemp thing has exploded into something

more . . . spiritual?" said DBO. "Some say the women honor the hemp way too much, but not Verruca—she says it's way more than a plant."

Vegas, hell-bent on getting through the greenhouse as quickly as possible, huffed a "Let's get on"; the smell was particularly bad that day.

DBO, ignoring the "let's get on," continued. "She says recycling here is way beyond anything you can imagine, and as for the robots?"

Vegas holding her nose, stopped. "Just exactly who is this Verruca?"

DBO was about to explain, hopefully with some sort of *capow!* at the end, when her earphones pinged.

"What was that?" said Vegas, trying not to breathe through her nose.

"Verruca. Apparently, they are staying in the dormitories."

"Don't they always?" said Vegas.

"Not the Voted In, the Operators," said DBO.

"What? Then where are the Voted In?"

"Stationaries," said DBO.

"Stationaries?" said Vegas. "What on Earth . . ."

DBO chuckled. "No, they are in the basement . . . apparently wearing bras."

"Who, the Voted In or the Operators?" said Vegas.

"The Voted In," muttered DBO.

Vegas tried to imagine a Voted In on a stationary in a bra and giggled.

"And the Operators are . . ." DBO stopped to listen. "Swapping suits . . . silks? And they still have no idea I am missing . . . or H2."

"How could anyone not miss you?" muttered Vegas.

Pope watched as DBO approached.

"Is that her then?" he muttered.

"Looks like it," said Prudence.

"Who else would it be?" said Pot.

"She's a bit small," said Pope, "and awfully young—do you think she is up for the task?"

"She better be," said Pot. "That Deidre is sniffing around."

"She's just a reporter, who listens to her?" said Pope.

"Well, everyone," said Prudence.

It took Hilda several reads of the leaflet to understand her drill was anything but a drill. She was not used to happiness; in fact, she had no real concept of it, and she found it hard to understand the need for such an instrument, but as Alice left with a quiet click of the door, Hilda turned on the drill.

"Best in bed," said the leaflet. "Comfort being a premium."

Hilda turned her clock off and positioned herself as instructed, and then, before she knew it, her puff ball of a face, the exploding shed, and even Beryl was forgotten as Hilda, for the first time in her life, discovered there was more to life than ruining someone else's.

Chapter Six

CREDIT NOTES

"The temperature of a room cannot always be measured with a thermometer." –The Chef, Planet Hy Man

It was agreed by all but Operator Four, who had been sent to the kitchen for a list, that two should head down to the basement to "destroy, deposit, or tweak," the H-Pad 11—and, whilst there, source "mending equipment, tools, and anything that would make this whole sad business easier."

Operator Two muttered about things being "a tad vague," but as the rest were arguing over who was going where, she decided to shut up with another scone firmly in place.

"Why don't you use the H-Pad 11 template?" said the secretary, who was also now the minute taker until they could source a mechanical one. "After all, that was the whole idea of pilfering it."

"You mean steal," said Operator Two.

Operator One told Operator Two to shut up, causing Operator Two to also shove a scone—cream overflowing—into her mouth.

"Perhaps we could use it to tweak, so to speak," said the secretary. She rolled out her template with an expectant "ta-da" look.

Operator One surveyed the template. "Don't minute this," she said to the secretary. "But this template idea is a good one."

"And perhaps," said the secretary, "after a bit of tweaking, the new H-Pad could take the minutes for us." She laughed.

"Yes, and if it *all* goes pear shaped, tits up, down the swanny, or just bomb, it'll be on your shoulders," said Operator Two with a spray of scone.

"At least I had the foresight to make a template—did any of you?" huffed the secretary.

Silence.

"And if you did think such an idea, would you be able to make one?"

The Operators shifted uncomfortably; there had been a few caustic comments about the template, which now, spread out on the table with impressive detail, seemed . . . well . . . bitchy.

"Didn't think so," said the secretary with a sniff.

"It's a nice template," muttered Operator One.

"Definitely," said Operator Three.

They both looked at Operator Two.

"Yes, it is," she mumbled.

"Thank you," said the secretary with a crisp rolling up of her template.

"Now, who's going to the basement?" said Operator One.

"How about Operator Four?" said Operator Two with a lick of her lips.

"But she's not here," said Operator One.

"Exactly," muttered Operator Two.

Operator Four burst in the door with a shopping list as long as a footman's arm. She spread it out on the table, and the Operators stared at it.

"Pickling podcasts, where's the funds for all that?" snapped Operator One.

"We're to barter," muttered Operator Four.

"Barter with what?"

"Credit notes, whatever that is," said Operator Four.

The secretary, sensing that credit notes and bartering was more complicated than the list spread out on the table, jumped in.

"I'll go to the basement."

"Me too," said Operator Four.

❄

When Operator One and Two left for the market, Operator Three stayed behind to, as Operator One and Two put it, "guard things."

With no idea exactly what she was to guard, Operator Three felt at a loose end. She had never been alone before; none of the Operators had. An Operator's childhood was spent in the Hatchery, outbuildings of the Compound (Planet Hy Man's answer to an orphanage), until they were old enough to work in places like the shed.

Operators were always together; they slept, ate, and argued together until too old to work and then shuffled to the "outer areas" or "outskirts," where women like Verruca lived; dusty, shady places, overgrown with trees and ivy, and the perfect place for annoying, out-of-date robots.

Operator Three stared at the opulent surroundings. What was she to do? How did guarding work?

She wandered about the corridor and in and out of each room, then headed into the kitchen . . .

Perhaps a beverage in one of those posh mugs Operator One hogged, or a long foot soak finished with a fluffy towel?

There was a ton of towels to choose from, stacked in color-coded piles. She ran her hands along the top of the shag-pile towels, drinking in the luxurious scent. Where she came from, towels were harsh hemp affairs that left scratch marks on your skin.

She pressed a thick purple towel against her cheek. *These towels caress the skin.* She pondered the feel of it on her cracked heels and was just in the process of slipping off her shoe when Alice crashed through the barrack door and flew down the corridor.

"Meetings, meetings—must be arranged, must be arranged."

Operator Three slid the towel back in its place and headed into the corridor, stopping Alice midway.

"Meeting?" said Operator Three.

"Yes, bribery and corruption—must be sorted."

"By who?" said Operator Three.

"You," said Alice.

"Me?"

"You're the only one here," said Alice.

"But what do I know about sorting? And what about Hilda?"

"Hilda is on holiday," said Alice.

"Oh, forgot about that," muttered Operator Three.

Hilda, engrossed in her "drill," was on more than a holiday; she was, as they say on Earth, "on another planet" and had no intentions of leaving.

After a test run on her drill (she didn't dare call it anything else), Hilda let out a manic laugh, jolting her personal footman awake. Charging out of her room looking somewhat like a banshee, she tossed a list of orders at Alice and a copy at her personal footman.

"Here, put that in your oil filter and filter it!" She laughed.

"Filters are obsolete, ma'am," muttered her personal footman, averting his eyes.

"Figure of speech," cackled Hilda and, without even waiting for an answer, returned to her bedroom.

She had switched off her H-Pad, turned off the lights, and left everything to know-it-all Alice. If she had to hide away from her world, then she may as well make a meal of it, and what better way to make a meal of it than with this so-called drill?

Alice lifted her list. "Robots don't do figures of speech," she muttered.

"Neither do footman," said the personal footman.

Operator Three, with one last look at the piles of towels, headed to the room with a view. She had no idea what to do, but she knew it all started in the room with a view.

She wondered about sorting . . . she could shuffle things about, have a rummage, or source information, at least until the others got back.

She stopped mid corridor.

But what if they didn't? What if she was left all on her own?

She looked about.

Surely not?

The footmen lining the corridor watched, stifling their amusement. They had seen that look on any number of Voted Ins.

By the time she arrived at the room with a view, a report was on the table and Alice was circling the room.

Turns out there had been a run of pilfering in the marketplace, and some were blaming the mice. Operator Three agreed that there seemed to be a lot of them, and she asked Alice if she had a plan.

When Alice motioned a "no," Operator Three thought for a minute.

"I could organize a meeting," she said, "and . . ." She jumped at her brilliance. "The secretary could take minutes."

"How is that going to help?" said Alice.

Operator Three slumped. "You're right; it's just that I am used to thinking with others. Bouncing ideas, we call it."

She sighed and then looked at Alice. "Do you fancy a bounce . . . of ideas?"

Alice said nothing.

"I mean in the shed we just sort of fed the mice and they'd go away."

"Fed mechanical mice?" said Alice.

Alice, like those she served, lived high above the ground and had never seen a mouse.

"Yes," said Operator Three. "They have mutated, taken to nibbling, usually on material like our disposable cups. When there was a lull, we used to set up trails leading to traps."

She smiled to herself. *The good old shed days . . .* She stopped.

"We could make one in the marketplace: an entrapment with materials."

"*Entrapment* is not a great name," said Alice.

Operator Three looked excited.

"We could make a paper trail—they use paper in the market, don't they?"

She paused, took some notes, then looked at Alice.

"We could lead the mice outside the market."

She stopped and clapped her hands.

"What about the Black Hills? I have read about them. We could send them there."

Alice silently processed the plan. She could see many flaws and was just about to elaborate when Operator Three grabbed her hand and shook it.

"Thanks, Alice, you've been a big help."

"But I didn't do . . ." Alice stopped. "All in a day's work, ma'am."

"Now what do we do?" said Operator Three.

"I think the next step is implementation," muttered a footman.

Chapter Seven

DEIDRE

"For society to survive, the invisible are needed." –The Cleaners' Manual

Deidre had been a reporter since she was old enough to snoop and write. To her, anyone was fair game, which was probably why she had no friends.

She said she was born to tell what must be told. Others, questioning the whole "tell what must be told" theory, called her a cold, calculating chancer with no shame, some even to her face. She didn't care; she lived for the next story. But today was different . . .

While Vegas and DBO were making their way through the greenhouse and Hilda was inspecting her "drill," Deidre's mind was working overtime. She had a feeling in her reporter bones, a feeling that caused her indigestion. The last time she'd felt like that was when she heard of the mechanical parrots.

She was sitting at her desk at the time, staring out onto the courtyard of greatness.

In the past, she had written for Beryl. In fact, the rise of Beryl was the making of Deidre, and her chronicling of man's downfall was her finest work.

"They cannot adapt," she wrote, "and you'd think they would. They are still trying to fix things, claiming to be invaluable even though robots can do a much better job *and* with a foot rub into the bargain."

Thanks to Deidre, the fall of man was swift. She'd even helped to smooth over the whole mechanical parrot episode. She, free of charge, collected data knowing that later the data would come in handy.

She was still waiting . . .

When Beryl's power began to wane, Deidre callously looked elsewhere, and it wasn't long before she was seduced by Hilda, although it didn't take much persuading. Hilda was a generous briber, while Beryl expected loyalty on a shoestring.

They met weekly in the spa, Hilda lending Deidre her soft towels and sharing her sparkling water. In fact, it was in the spa that they'd had their last conversation, just before the disappearance of Beryl.

Hilda had taken her by surprise.

The spa was extra luxurious that day, the water fragrant with seductive hemp oil, the sparkly extra chilled. For the first time ever, a footman was ordered to rub not only Hilda's shoulders but Deidre's as well, and while he worked on the knots on Deidre's neck, Hilda talked of the futility of voting, and how one could not expect the masses to grasp what was in the planet's best interest.

"They believe anyone in a white coat," said Hilda, "especially when quoting figures. And they don't even have to understand the figures."

"Perhaps you underestimate the masses," said Deidre.

Hilda laughed, slid under the water, and returned, hair spiky, a signal for Deidre to nod a yes.

When Deidre did, Hilda topped up her glass. She waved the footman away and he, with great ceremony, bowed and backed away into a corner.

No one noticed.

"The masses are not fit to choose a leader," Hilda said. "And someone like you can help ease the transition."

A sense of unease hit Deidre; she knew what transition meant.

"My stories are not that popular," she muttered. "I mean transition requires more than a few stories, loyalty for a start."

"But they are not stories," said Hilda, "are they? And being disliked —sorry, hated—is a bonus."

Deidre muttered a "Thanks."

"Look at me." Hilda smiled. "Being obeyed does not require friendship, merely fear, and fear unites the masses."

Deidre sipped her sparkly. It was beginning to lose its taste. She felt she had no choice but to follow Hilda into whatever she had planned. And now, as she looked at her H-Pad, she wondered just when she was going to hear of said plan.

That night, Vegas and DBO sat by the fire on the veranda with the three robots, DBO finally silent.

DBO loved the greenhouse. She was so engrossed in the plants she didn't notice the smell, and once she saw the recycling pit, she could not contain herself and bombarded the robots with so many questions that even the robots got tired of talking—and they loved talking. Finally, they dragged her off to the veranda, filled her with biscuits and hot hemp chocolate, and lit a fire. It didn't take long for DBO to stop talking.

She listened to the mechanical katydids and crickets filling the dark with songs. She had never heard anything so peaceful in her life and messaged Verruca, "What a truly beautiful evening."

"Most of us only remembered what crickets looked like, some even painted them, but no one knew they could be reinvented until *she* came along," said Prudence.

"She?" muttered Vegas.

"Yes, *he* was a master of spark plugs," muttered Pope, "but *she* knew so much more."

"She?" said Vegas and DBO in unison.

Prudence tapped her nose. "All in good time."

"Hate it when they do that," muttered Vegas to DBO.

Deidre planted herself at the foot of Hilda's unfinished statue in the courtyard of greatness and inhaled the night air.

Her feet ached.

She had spent all day searching every place she could think of and she was still no further forward. She had investigated, eavesdropped, even attempted a bit of bribery, and the only thing for sure was that Hilda was incognito and the whole city was bubbling in excited ignorance.

That morning, Deidre, like most who worked in the Building of Opulence, lined up for her fried tofu roll in the canteen and was stunned into silence. An unfamiliar buoyant mood filled the room; there was laughing, joshing, and women lounging about the tables toasting "let's hear it for Hilda." Even the plate clearers seemed in a festive mood.

Deidre was speechless.

The canteen was usually a somber place of moans about "the mice size portions" and "lukewarm beverages"; toasting was as rare on Planet Hy Man as a plate of bacon and a full stomach as hard to come by as a shag. Not that Deidre had any idea what that was . . .

In fact, the last time Deidre remembered toasting was when Legless broke the hundred-mile record on his stationary and Beryl, with a rare smile, called an afternoon off for *all* in the Building of Opulence.

And that wasn't yesterday.

Deidre stood in the queue watching a jubilant serving robot tossing extra tofu and sauce on a roll with no care of the budget.

What the pickle was going on?

"Hilda is on holiday," said the robot, attempting to squash the jam-packed roll into submission.

"Yay!" said a woman from behind.

"Tuck in," said another.

"Holiday?" said Deidre. "That is the stupidest thing I have ever heard. Hilda couldn't make it through an hour without issuing an order; she'd die if she couldn't interfere, or at least have a panic attack."

"Well, apparently she is breathing, sunning, and relaxing by the seaside," said the serving robot.

"I would query seaside," muttered Deidre.

"It was on the morning screen," said the woman from behind.

"The woman in the white coat was quite explicit," said another.

Deidre stopped. "No Hilda onscreen?"

"*Sooo*," said the serving robot, thrusting a roll bulging with tofu at Deidre, "tuck in."

Deidre's suspicions began to gnaw her insides.

Every morning, Hilda appeared on public screens all over the city. She liked to start the day reminding the masses of all she had done for them, following it up with a list of orders. Hilda lived and breathed her work; there was nothing she liked better than issuing orders, and she'd never use the lady-in-a-white-coat hologram.

It was a Beryl initiative.

"Hilda's experimenting," said the woman.

"With a view to rolling out breaks, holidays, *and* possible sick leave," said the robot.

"Ahhh, the luxury of healing in bed," said a plate cleaner.

"Apparently, they are all the rage on Earth," said another.

"Considered a necessary," said the robot. "For optimum performance."

A few chuckled.

Hurrah!

Get stuck in.

Deidre finished her roll in silence. There was something fishy. She decided to head over to the lobby of clerks; perhaps they would make more sense.

Chapter Eight

THE GARDEN OF GREATNESS

"The illusion of being heard keeps peace." —Scribbled under the Voted In's table

Deidre spent the morning loitering incognito style by water coolers and beverage centers. She started in the lobby of the Building of Opulence and, hearing nothing but "Let's put our feet up" and "Fancy another sparkly," moved on to the cleaner's and limo mechanic's lounge. Everyone was in a jubilant spirit. It seemed Hilda's holiday was front-page news, and she—Hilda's right-hand reporter—knew nothing about it. Had she been dropped?

Exhausted, confused, and a little panicky, she arrived at the courtyard of greatness just as the sun was setting. Hilda usually appeared at the end of the day to view the artist's work; she liked to hear what the artist had to say while sharing an evening beverage.

Tonight, Deidre waited in the shadows. No one appeared.

She stared up at the unfinished Hilda statue. It was carved from recycled material and looked impressively large, especially the nose. She was just thinking of calling it a day when she noticed a footman dragging a rake into the courtyard.

She caught his eye.

"She's been and gone," he said.

"What?"

"The artist."

"And Hilda?"

The footman shook his head. "Only Alice."

"Alice was here?" Deidre stopped. *Hilda only used Alice for, well . . . emergencies.*

"Left a note," shouted the footman.

"A note?"

"Pissed the artist right off. Said the nose was too big."

"Too big."

"As large as an elephant's penis." He paused. "To quote her."

Deidre looked up at Hilda's nose. She had never seen an elephant, let alone a penis.

"I mean look at it." The footman gestured with his rake. "You could ski on that thing."

"Ski?" said Deidre. "On a penis?"

The footman eyed Deidre. "You're that reporter?"

She said nothing.

"Looking for a story, I suppose."

"Might be," said Deidre.

The footman began to rake the gravel. "Strange days when the great Deidre comes here looking for a story."

"Whose says I am looking?" said Deidre.

The footman leaned on his rake. "Everyone."

"Hardly everyone."

"I heard you didn't even know about the holiday," said the footman.

"Did too."

"Called it malarkey," said the footman.

"Did not."

"What's all this holiday malarkey about? That's what you said." The footman continued to rake. "Mind you that Hilda would never take a day off—she's as much chance of taking a holiday as you have of skiing on that pickling nose up there."

"Exactly," said Deidre.

"Strange times," he muttered.

Deidre waited . . . silence always led to talk.

She watched as the footman circled the rake about the gravel, creating swirly patterns.

"Operators in the marketplace," he said. "Did you ever hear of such a thing?"

She waited . . .

"Bartering."

Silence . . .

"I mean an Operator with a list from the kitchen, what's that about?" said the footman.

"What?" said Deidre.

The footman continued to swirl. "Going around asking where do I get herbal hemp and how much is a handful? I mean what's an Operator to know about such things?"

"Shouldn't they be in the shed?" said Deidre.

"*And* making a complete balls-up." The footman stopped. "No idea how to barter."

"I heard Hilda's getting about in scarves," said Deidre.

"Scarves? Hilda?"

"Yeah, like a terrorist."

The footman stopped, leaned on his rake, and looked at her. "That is what the Operators say."

"And how would they know?" said Deidre.

"The kitchen," said the footman.

Deidre stopped. "Kitchen?"

"It was a list for the kitchen," said the footman. He looked at her with an isn't-it-obvious stance . "Probably where the whole scarf story started."

Deidre looked at him. There was nothing more annoying than a footman with an isn't-it-obvious stance.

"I mean it's as plain as that nose on Hilda's face," he muttered.

Deidre stood at the kitchen door, unable to enter; it was blocked by a cleaner robot droning "No visitors" in a monotonous tone while clutching a broom like the Sword of Damocles.

Behind the door was Lilia, the assistant, and the cook, who talked like she was in the middle of a field a mile from her audience. In truth, she had an earwax problem and refused any sort of cleaning, claiming that "nature was a better healer than any idiot robot with a syringe."

A sentiment many of a certain age agreed with.

"I knew it wouldn't be long before the Operators would cock it up. I mean drinking caffeine takes practice," said the cook.

"And brains," said Lilia.

"It's a mess," said the cook.

"Hello? Can I come in?" shouted Deidre.

The cook looked at Lilia. "Is someone at the door?"

The robot, with a menacing wave of his broom, said, "Yes . . . she's asking questions."

"Is that Deidre?" yelled the cook.

"I just want a word," shouted Deidre.

"No thanks," said the cook.

The cook had heard that Deidre was on the prowl, and the last person she wanted sniffing out stories was her. She had a deep dislike for motormouth Deidre ever since her scathing "it was a scone but not as we know it" article.

The last thing they needed was a Deidre article, the cook had been warned . . .

"If any of this gets out," slurred Hilda, "your parts will be hung out to dry. And drying parts is way more painful than robots with syringes."

The cook looked at the door. She was fond of her parts.

"Just a quick word about scarves and things," said Deidre.

"I know nothing," said the cook.

"Bet you do."

"I'll tell you what I do know," shouted the cook. "Your spa meetings with Herself the leader—everyone knows about them."

"They weren't a secret," Deidre lied.

"And now *she's* vanished," shouted the cook. "Folk think you got something to do with it."

The robot nodded, gesturing with his broom for Deidre to leave.

"Well I haven't, and you can tell whoever is spreading *that* rumor—"

"No one spreading rumors, it's organic," shouted the cook.

"Organic? What in the pickled gherkin is that supposed to mean?" said Deidre.

The robot gave her another shove with his broom.

"Can you call this idiot off?" shouted Deidre.

The cook was silent.

"You're not welcome here," snapped the robot. "You are bad news."

Deidre heard a door slam, a rustling of bags, followed by a different voice.

"Shush, she'll hear," said Lilia.

"What's going on in there?" snapped Deidre.

"Nothing," shouted the two cooks in unison.

"Nothing," shouted an unknown voice.

"Shhhh," hissed another unknown voice.

Deidre looked at the robot; he gestured menacingly with his broom. Deidre grabbed the broom, shooed the robot, and entered the kitchen.

She stopped . . .

In front of her were two Operators clutching shopping bags of food with a shameful look like they had been caught pilfering.

"Shouldn't you be in the shed?" she said. Then, catching sight of the garden through the patio doors, she gasped.

There was a black patch where the shed used to be, with one footman stumbling about with a rake and another attempting to pick up rubble at a snail's pace.

What the pickle . . . was going on?

Chapter Nine

THE FALLING OF A FOOTMAN

"Ours is not to question why but to tuck in before we die." –The Chef's Assistant

After several futile discussions, followed by incomprehensible directions from one of the footmen, it was agreed that the footman with the incomprehensible directions should accompany Operator Four and the secretary to the basement.

He was a man of annoying comments and squeaky farts who moved with a shuffle that exasperated the two women. They followed with suppressed impatience as the footman dawdled through several corridors, various doors, sharp turns, and a tunnel, frequently stopping to catch his breath. Finally arriving at a door with a red light above and "The Basement" scrawled across, they stopped.

The footman, with a grunt, attempted to push the door open. It was a tough door, jammed at the bottom. The footman bent to unjam the door, squeaking a fart in the process.

The secretary let out an "Oh for pickle's sake" sigh.

Operator Four, pushing the footman out the way with a "here, let me," handed him the deluxe headphones.

As she opened the door, a robust fart echoed through the corridor door, the deeper tones stopping her in her tracks.

She shot a look at the footman.

"Wasn't me," snorted the footman. He turned to the secretary.

"Me neither," she snapped.

Another fart ripped through the air.

"More of a tone from Earth?" muttered the footman.

The secretary looked at the deluxe headphones. A barking noise started . . .

"Possibly a dog?" he added.

They listened as more unfamiliar sounds came from the earphones: tin opening, scraping, plopping, followed by slurping and silence.

"A headset, but not as we know it," chuckled the footman.

"They are headphones," said Operator Four as the secretary, snatching the headphones from the footman, told him to wait at the door.

The women headed into the basement . . .

Deidre stood in the kitchen, watching the footman bend to pick up what looked like a large bedspring; he was so frail he looked like he would snap at the hips.

He stumbled.

Deidre gasped.

The footman teetered.

"How old is he?" said Deidre.

No one answered. The cook, tutting, was busy unpacking the grocery bags. She looked at the two Operators.

"How much did you pay for this?"

Operator One mumbled a price.

The footman righted himself with a wobble, preparing for another bend.

"I mean should he be doing that?" said Deidre.

The robot, with a broom now uselessly brushing about the pantry, looked up. "It's all in the training."

The cook tutted at Operator Two. "Have you not heard of bartering?"

"We bartered," said Operator One with a sheepish look.

The cook, with a shake of her head, weighed a packet of hemp flour in her hand. "You were robbed."

Lilia and the kitchen porter, with a smug "thank pickle it's not me" look, shooed the robot away and began to pack the groceries into the pantry.

"He's gonna fall," yelled Deidre.

"Leave him," yelled the cook.

The kitchen porter, with a crisp folding of an empty grocery bag, looked up. "They *are* trained," she tutted.

Lilia nodded at the Operators. "Falling to them is a piece of pickle."

"More a collapsing," muttered the kitchen porter. She turned to the Operators. "You ever seen a footman collapse?"

The Operators shook their heads.

"Like a pack of cards," she said.

"A concertina?" said Lilia.

"Concertina?" said Operator One.

The footman teetered into a bend. His heels lifted; he righted himself until his toes lifted.

He wobbled.

"He's gonna go," shouted Deidre.

The other footman in the garden leaned on his rake, watching like it was a comedy act.

The footman balanced himself, stopped, stared at the spring, and then made for it *again!*

"Leave it," shouted Deidre. She looked around at the unmoved mob. "Does no one care?"

The footman faltered.

Deidre, opening the window, shouted, "I'll get it!"

The footman stopped, attempted a head turn towards *the voice*, overbalanced, and crashed to the ground.

"Bugger," he muttered.

"Drama queen," sighed the footman with the rake.

"That's what comes of interfering," muttered the kitchen porter. "You bugger up the whole collapsing process."

The cook, with a glare at Deidre, muttered, "Told her, but would she listen? Just like that Hilda."

Deidre stopped. "Hilda?"

"Did I say Hilda?" muttered the cook.

As the footman stood on guard outside the basement, the secretary and Operator Four entered and, like Hilda and Beryl before them, walked past the *buggered equipment* shelf, the *you're having a laugh* equipment display, and the *when men ruined the planet* sections.

In fact, they were sure they could detect not only a slight whiff of Beryl's hairspray but Hilda's nonfragrant underarm freshener, a strange mixture of caffeine and almond.

The basement was a cold, dark place. There was one lightbulb above the entrance, which with the right power lit the basement up like the midday sun. However, thanks to the basement being at the end of the lighting loop, and the Voted In's spurts of speed followed by "joshing" breaks, the lightbulb had been working overtime and now had light on par with a pocket torch with "done" batteries.

Operator Four and the secretary had made their way to the recycling area at the back of the basement and, in the shadows, tripped on a good old-fashioned plug.

The secretary tutted.

They peered into the same shelves of obsolete phones and cameras that Hilda and Beryl looked at, finally coming to what they were searching for: the C-Pad shelf.

A mechanical mouse flashed past as the light flickered off and on.

The secretary rolled out her template on the floor. The mechanical mouse appeared, skidding on the template; the secretary brushed it aside. It skidded across the floor like a shoe on ice.

"We need this"—she pointed—"and this and this, but not this."

The light flicked off. They stopped, the secretary on all fours over her template.

They waited.

A mouse rustled past, followed by another . . .

They waited.

"I suppose I have to do it in the dark," muttered Operator Four.

"What?" said the secretary. She was sure something had just nipped her hand.

"Rummage," said Operator Four.

The secretary, rubbing her hand, nodded in the dark. "Mind the mice."

The Operator stretched her arm to the back of the shelf and, brushing the mechanical mouse dust, began to rummage. She pulled at something sharp, metallic; there was a clatter as something crashed onto her foot.

"What the pickle," she muttered.

The light flashed on, and she looked at a mechanical rat the size of a cat on her foot. She pushed it with her toe under the bottom shelf.

The secretary stood up. "Where are all these mice coming from?"

Squeak . . .

"I have no idea," said the Operator.

Rustle . . .

Another loud fart erupted from the headphones, followed by a yawn and a licking sound.

"Not me," shouted the footman.

The secretary examined the headphones, looking for a volume control.

"The H-Pad II controls the volume," said Operator Four, giving the shelf another go with a grunt. Mouse dust tumbled to the floor.

The secretary turned the decapitated H-Pad II in her hands and muttered a "Hmmm."

Her hands grew sweaty.

The H-Pad II flashed on.

"Bugger, forgot about the whole body-fluids thing," muttered the secretary.

"What?" said Operator Four with another grunt.

"The saliva and body fluid, how it can ignite connections."

The secretary began to fumble with the decapitated H-Pad II as the two pieces tried to draw together like magnets.

"I can't stop it."

Operator Four turned and looked at the secretary vainly trying to keep the two sections apart.

The secretary looked at Operator Four. "Who the hell came up with the body-fluids thing?"

"Drop it, let the sweat dry," shouted the footman, "always works where I come from."

The two Operators looked at each other. "Works where I come from?" mouthed Operator Four.

"No idea," mouthed the secretary and, with a "worth a try" shrug, dropped the H-Pad 11.

The two pieces crashed to the floor and immediately clicked together.

"Oh," muttered Operator Four.

"Bugger," said the footman.

The H-Pad 11, firing up, began to circle on the spot. It lifted into the air like a miniature spaceship as a pencil, sharpened to a point, protruded from the center.

"Bollocking pickle," muttered Operator Four.

Chapter Ten

HILDA AND THE DRILL

"The speed of a drill is not necessarily the most important thing." –Plumber unknown

While Deidre was trying to come to terms with an out-of-action Hilda, Verruca was in her kitchen polishing the surface of her out-of-date table.

Verruca was the most underestimated woman on the planet who, yet again, had the future of the planet in the palm of her gnarled hands.

She had been part of the hippie movement; she'd helped when the digital tidy-up age came into being. She diverted as they copied the written word, hid books, squirrelled away parts of the libraries as they were being torn down. Verruca was a master of diversion, and when the hippies left to set up their new colony, it was she who diverted so well no one noticed.

She still missed the library—staring at books, flicking pages in a quiet place, even the smell of old paper—but she never regretted staying. She knew that somewhere in the future there would be more diverting needed. She stared at her shed. Now it was time to do it all over again.

Finding a "clear out the attic" job for her robot, which would keep him occupied *for decades*, she had secured her screen on the fridge and was flicking from one scene to the next, watching the planet.

She, thanks to a cobbled-together spy system, had full view of most places on the planet despite the fact that the system had been made from scrap scavenged away in her shed. Verruca had boxes full of equipment from the good old days when women conquered men. Over the years, she had pilfered it all, even the first mechanical homing pigeon template, and created a state-of-the-art system that any intelligence team would give their secret password for.

Verruca was a genius, a testament to maturity, that old age achieved on plant food really did keep the brain cells ticking—well, that and a lot of tinkering. Tinkering, according to Verruca, kept the brain cells active, and she tinkered like there was no tomorrow, creating equipment which, thanks to Hilda's so-called holiday, she could use to save her beloved planet.

"Tinkering," said Verruca, "is an octogenarian's right hand."

Not that anyone listened, apart from the mechanical mice rustling about her shed.

Occasionally the mice ventured into the house, causing great squealing, frantic broom waving, and serious object throwing from the robot. As soon as the robot saw a mouse dashing across the floor, he was up on a chair throwing anything he could lay his hands on. It was the best part of having a robot, thought Verruca, until he lobbed a tomato; the mess took ages to clean up.

Verruca finished her polishing and sat down. She stared at the screen, taking notes.

Vegas and DBO on the veranda with robots.

Deidre in the kitchen, awareness of the exploding shed taking time to settle in.

Hilda alone with a package.

The Voted In nicely preoccupied.

A mouse squeaked out from under the fridge. She dropped her pen and smiled.

"Now all I have to do is connect the kitchen to the veranda and"—she tossed a corner of paper near the mouse—"trust in the genius of DBO and H2."

She sat back with a smile. Her prodigies could handle anything.

The Voted Ins had taken to writing and drawing, after a shift on a stationary. It was Baby who started it; she started with new bra designs and then moved on to drawing cartoons of the cooks in the kitchen from her window. The others soon followed. There was little else to do, and they had so much energy; besides, they wanted something on the walls apart from the poster of fifties women.

Who needed to look at that in their twilight years?

They started with memories of the room with the view, scenes from their old window, but soon, inspired by Baby's "cooks of the kitchen" cartoon series, moved onto the odd portrait.

They fought over who to paint; most wanted to draw Voted In One, as she had the ability to stand still and gaze like no other. With just one glance she could look insightful, intelligent, or, if asked, innocent, like "one of those deer we used to see," and she could keep it up for hours without a wobble.

Soon their barracks was a place to behold, a place to enjoy, and they got so carried away that at times they forgot about their cycling only to jump on and cycle like mad, sending the energy levels soaring.

The cleaners had their work cut out for them. Managing the Voted In's energy burst was not easy until the Voted In ran out of drawing implements.

Then the power shifted . . .

Once Hilda flicked on the drill, Verruca flicked on the heat-sensory mode in Hilda's penthouse. She did have some discretion, and the last thing she wanted to see was Hilda getting to grips with her so-called drill . . .

Capturing the heat of Hilda was enough for Verruca to know Hilda's whereabouts. And, just for backup, she had installed a speaker in the attic and programmed her robot for ear alert to any talk of Hilda leaving her pad.

Surely he couldn't balls that up?

She poured a weak cup of beverage, sipped, pulled a *yuck* face, skulled it, and pondered DBO's message. *So there were crickets somewhere.* She looked out onto the garden. *An evening is not complete without the sound of a cricket, and as for a katydids* . . . She sighed and was just conjuring moments spent under the spell of a katydids song when she spied the robot shoving bags of who knows what into the shed . . .

She opened the window. "What are you up to?"

The robot stopped like he had been caught with his hand in a biscuit jar and then tried to slip behind a hedge.

"No point hiding, I have seen you."

"I am not here." Said the robot.

DBO drank in knowledge like Hilda drank in fear, and Vegas was seriously threatened. She thought she was intelligent, and yet keeping up with Ms Wonder Woman's mind was as easy as staggering through the Black Hills in silk slippers.

Not that she had them anymore, or her silk suit. She, now wearing the scratchy yet easy-to-get-about hemp "leisure suit," looked like a local and was accepted as one when she ceremonially tossed her silks onto the recycling heap.

The alterations team hadn't seen silk in years and spent hours rubbing it against their skin, arguing over what it should be, not to mention who should make it into what it should be; until, that is, they remembered that silk slipped like oil between the fingers and was "a bastard to sew."

"A sheet," said one.

"Or a set of pillowcases," said another.

"And then we all could have a shot," suggested another.

Chapter Eleven

CONTACT

"Great contact is not always visible." −Alice

Once Verruca had made contact with DBO, she was unstoppable. Bombarding the robots—who, for the most part, were happy to take things a tad slower—with questions, DBO bled them dry with queries. She wanted to know all about recycling and energy from water, wind, and could the power be used on a larger scale?

Finally exasperated, Pope turned to the mountain of books littered on the veranda, telling DBO to "knock herself out," and when that didn't keep her quiet, they took her to the café.

The alterations team, who in the end agreed on pillowcases, had invited Vegas and her team for "a slap-up chocolate session"—a thank-you for the silk. And Pope figured if the Alterationist didn't shut her up (they could talk a H-Pad to sleep), the hot chocolate would. It was the best hot chocolate on the planet, silencing sippers with a "hmmm" that lasted for ages; too good to gulp, let alone talk over.

DBO, wiping chocolate from her mouth, looked around at the café.

It was like a cave painted in bright colors. The walls were made from recycled rubber, a material that had not been used for centuries. The rubber had been molded to look like stone and painted with recycled glass water pipes winding their way through the walls like ivy on a tree. The water bubbled like a brook which lulled a woman under the influence of hot chocolate into a state of "who cares." And if that was not hypnotic enough, there were *real* fish mellowing in tanks under the counter.

DBO, attempting to focus, pulled out a pad and pen while Vegas and the 33 Robots, having finished their hot chocolate, decided the only thing to do was order more.

Hemp chocolate had that effect.

It was so delicious you had to have more, and the more you had, the less inclined you felt to do anything apart from drink more . . . which led to smiling, listening to your heartbeat, and gazing.

Chocolate lingered on Vegas's tongue as she gazed into the fish tank.

"Chill," muttered Pot.

"Relax," sighed Vegas, running her finger around the rim of the mug and then gulping her chocolate.

DBO stopped as an extra jug of hot chocolate appeared on the table. "What are you doing? You can't operate and drink that stuff, let alone think."

Vegas stopped mid sip. "Who's talking of operating, let alone thinking?" She gestured with the hot chocolate jug. "More?"

"More? We need to set up camp," said DBO, "make the most of this dip."

"Dip? Camp? What are you on about?" said Pope.

"Hilda's incognito with some sort of drill thing . . ."

Vegas shifted uncomfortably.

". . . so we can't waste time. I mean *she* has the concentration of a robot."

"Thanks."

"I mean the original robot—with old-fashioned dials."

"We all have to start somewhere," muttered Prudence.

"Well, the concentration of a footman then," muttered DBO.

"That's ageist that is," muttered a particularly wrinkled Alterationist. "You try standing all day in out-of-date pseudo-silk, it sweats like a bastard."

DBO, with an "I hear you comrade" nod, continued.

"As I said, we have a dip and need to make use of it. I mean Hilda's hardly going to be playing this drill thing for long."

"Drill," snorted the elderly Alterationist, "is that what you call it?"

The others laughed.

"You needn't worry about Hilda, she'll be gone for ages." Prudence patted DBO's hand.

"What?"

"Oh yeah, that *drill* will knock you out for hours," said Prudence. She looked at Vegas. "You should give her a shot of yours."

"I have offered," muttered Vegas, "but it seems the dip is of greater importance."

"A dip is merely a dip," muttered Pope.

DBO opened her notes. She had several diagrams and a map. The Alterationist peered over; the wrinkled one looked impressed.

"There is a lull in the power chain; the Voted In have taken to bras and drawing."

"Bras? Wouldn't mind a shot myself," said the waitress, pulling a "get a load of these" pose.

A few laughed.

"And a G-string," shouted a voice from the back, "what I would give for the discomfort of that!"

"*So-o-o*," continued DBO, "our main problem is to change the power without them knowing what's going on."

"Going on? What do you mean going on?"

"I know what's going on here," said the voice from the back with her version of the "get a load of these" pose.

DBO, with an exasperated sigh, continued. "The energy—you can't depend on stationaries for it, especially women that age."

"Ageist," snapped a voice from the back.

"We're fine here, who cares about them," muttered a robot wiping the counter.

"Yes, but you won't be *fine* if things get into a pickle over there, will you? If you want to protect *this*"—DBO gestured around the café—"then you have to fix *that*," she said, waving in the direction of the city.

The robot stopped mid wipe. "Oh."

"There is an energy crisis," said DBO. "And it's your problem too."

"We have wind scarecrows and real fish—what have we to worry about?" muttered the waitress with a quick rub of the fish tank.

DBO talked of the lost spark plug (which everyone knew about) and the inevitable "collapsing of the city under the stop-start energy of the Voted In. I mean how long is all this utopia of yours going to last if the energy in the city runs out?" said DBO. "Before you can say 'sew this,' they'll be rummaging through your precious library, confiscating your wind scarecrows . . ."

The women reluctantly listened.

"Aren't you being just a tad melodramatic?" said Prudence.

"Why don't we just lock the 'don't open' gate?" muttered Pot.

The H-Pad II lit up the basement, shining light onto piles of mechanical mouse dust and an Aladdin's cave of equipment, some dating as far back as when men made things.

The two Operators had never seen anything like it before.

"Illuminating," said the H-Pad II crisply.

A bark erupted from the headphones. The secretary, not knowing what else to do, gave the headphones a shake.

"It is but a mere dog, ma'am," said the H-Pad II. "From Earth."

"Oh, one of those," muttered Operator Four.

"And, with a few adjustments, we can expand the connection, explore . . . such fun." The H-Pad II began to buzz about the shelves, pointing its pencil. "Now all one needs is this, and . . . this, and . . . oh, yes, some of this would be marvelous."

Operator Four, getting into the swing of things, pulled out a set of roller skates (which she had never seen before). "What about this?"

The H-Pad II stopped. "Ma'am, those are but rolling implements, not required for the present mission."

"And this," said the secretary, pulling out an ancient H-Pad prototype.

"One H-Pad is enough, ma'am," snapped the H-Pad II, "now plug in that . . . no, not that . . . not that . . . I said *that*!"

"Apologies," muttered the secretary.

"And that!"

Operator Four jumped to attention.

"And . . ."

A mouse sauntered past. The H-Pad 11 took aim with her pencil; the mouse caught sight, scurried across the template, and, with a few skids, made it under a box.

The H-Pad 11 stopped. "The template—we have no need of this. Shall I dispose?"

The Operators looked at each other.

"Why don't we attach the headphones?" said the secretary to the H-Pad 11. "Get down to some expanding, you were talking about."

"What?" said the H-Pad 11.

"See what all those weird noises are about," added Operator Four.

"The tin opening?" said the H-Pad 11.

The Operators looked at each other. "Yes, the tin opening."

The H-Pad 11 tuned into Earth and zoomed in on Izzie, while the secretary scurried her template into the front of her pants.

"A small dog," said H-Pad 11. She listened. "Near the bin of a human . . . it has the remains of a . . ." H Pad 11 stopped. "Oh dear."

She flew to the door. "We need to head back to the room with a view, call a meeting."

The two Operators jumped to attention.

"And mind to sign the 'helping yourself' form as you leave or you'll be sent an invoice." The H-Pad 11 paused for a moment. "The . . . template?"

The Operators looked at each other.

"What template?" said the secretary.

"The template of me," said the H-Pad 11, "must be destroyed."

"Mice," said Operator Four, "nibble anything, nibble a footman's hanky if you let 'em."

The H-Pad 11 swirled around, pointing her pencil at the two Operators. "That template was mice-protected."

"Was it?" said Operator Four.

"Don't think so," said the secretary. "Can't have been."

"You sure?" said the H-Pad 11.

"Absolutely," said the two Operators.

Chapter Twelve

THE TICKLING OF AN H-PAD

"The pleasure of a scone is all in the topping." —Operator Three

When Deidre heard about Hilda and the shed, she, in a state of shock, took a seat. Clutching a glass of water, she asked, "Where is *she* now?"

The cook, engrossed in scone-dough rolling, shrugged. "Thought you with all your spa meetings would know—"

"Me?" said Deidre. "Hardly."

"—seeing as you're right up her goody-toes-shoes side and all."

Deidre coughed. "Hilda, goody-two-shoes side?" She let out a cynical chuckle. "That woman has no goody-two-shoes side, she is as tough as those burnt scones the birds have left."

The women stared at the hard-as-rock scones on the gravel.

"It was my first batch," muttered Lilia.

Operator One nudged Operator Two; her H-Pad was bleeping. "They have made it to the basement," she whispered.

The cook looked up. "Basement? Who's talking of the basement? That place is a trap just waiting to snap."

The Operators shuffled uncomfortably. "It's all a bit up in the air, what with the Voted In on stationaries," muttered Operator Four.

"And, well, Hilda's, err . . . accident," said Lilia.

The cook clipped her over the ear.

Lilia rubbed her ear.

"I thought she was on holiday," said Deidre.

"That is the accepted line," muttered the cook, resuming her dough rolling.

Operator One gestured to her H-Pad. "They have connected," she said. "To possibly a dog . . ."

"On Earth," Operator Two blurted.

"Give me that here," said Deidre.

Deidre stared at the H-Pad; two Operators blinked back, the secretary wearing the luxury earphones and Operator Four clutching an H-Pad 11 flashing like an ambulance in emergency mode.

Deidre stared at the H-Pad 11. "What sort of H-Pad is that? Drama queen variety?"

Operator One peered at the screen. "Shit, are they still using that thing?"

The secretary and Operator Four peered back. "It's a Hilda thing," shouted the secretary.

"And we're to exploit it," added Operator Four.

"Nobody said anything about exploiting," muttered Operator One. She looked at Deidre. "Definitely not me."

She peered back into the screen. "Thought we said to get rid of that so-called H-Pad."

"I am an H-Pad 11," said the H-Pad 11.

"I think the actual words were *recycle* and whatever . . ." said the secretary.

"Along with *indispose*"—Operator Four turned to the secretary—"or was it *predispose?*"

"Nothing was mentioned about recycling," snapped Operator Two.

"Yes it was," said the secretary.

"I think you'll find we talked of other *old* equipment, not that thing there," said Operator One.

"I'm still here," muttered the H-Pad 11.

"Pity," muttered Operator Two.

"And I am not recycled but rather refurbished," said the H-Pad 11.

"Scone?" said the cook to Deidre.

"You've got scones?" said the secretary. "All we've got is mice."

"What do you expect? It is a basement," the cook shouted at the H-Pad.

Deidre slid a scone into her mouth and, with an absent-minded *hmm*, began to think. *Earth? What do they want with Earth?*

The robot pushed his broom by Deidre's shoes with a "move your feet." Deidre jumped. "Why on Earth are we connected to . . . um . . . Earth?"

"It's a Beryl thing," muttered Operator Two.

"And we're to exploit it," shouted the secretary.

"Will you stop talking of exploiting?" snapped Operator One. "We are not a political organization."

"You sound like it," muttered the kitchen porter.

The cook, with a brisk wipe of the bench, snapped, "No one exploits anyone in this kitchen, we've elevenses to prepare. And that's not going to get done with your bollocking H-Pad talk."

"H-Pad 11!" snapped the H-Pad 11.

Deidre turned to Operator One. "Maybe you should tell me the whole thing."

"Not in here you're not. Off you go, and leave me and my kitchen in pickling peace—and keep your trap shut or I'll be ramming Lilia's scones down your throat."

"They were my first batch," sniffed Lilia.

In the end, Deidre, clutching a plate of rejected scones, followed the two Operators back to the room with a view. The Operators tried to argue but knew it was pointless: Deidre was as determined as Hilda, and she knew where to go. All journalists did.

***

"This way, ma'am," muttered the footman with a ceremonial gesture towards a corridor.

"There is a better way," said the H-Pad 11, shooting off in the other direction. She stopped and turned to the group. "Follow me, we'll be there in a shake of a cat's tail."

The secretary pulled a "cat's tail?" look at Operator Four.

"I saw that," said the H-Pad 11. "And I think you will find my satellite connections are far more efficient than the memory of an elderly footman." The H-Pad 11 turned to the footman. "No offense intended."

"None taken," muttered the footman.

Deidre and the Operators were already sitting around the large table arguing over whether minutes should be taken under the spy lock-down when the H-Pad 11 could be heard rattling about outside the door.

A footman entered. "Hear ye, hear ye, the right royal H-Pad 11 has arrived."

The H-Pad 11 zoomed into the room, the two Operators sheepishly following.

Operator One stood to attention. She had prepared a speech to put this upstart of an H-Pad 11 in its place. She pulled out her notes and looked about the room . . . "Before we start, we must be absolutely clear on the protocol of H-Pads, including"—she looked at the H-Pad 11—"any renovated, upcycled, or refurbished H-Pads."

The H-Pad 11 lit up . . . as ecstatic moaning came from the attached headphones.

"*Yes, yes, yes . . .*"

"Is that Hilda?" said Operator One.

"*Yeeeeeessss!!!!*"

The moans increased, accompanied by a robotic drilling noise in the background.

"Hilda, moan? The only time I heard her do that was when . . ." Operator Two stopped; it wasn't Hilda she'd heard moan.

Operator Four blushed.

The women stared at each other as the moaning continued. They felt like they were intruding . . .

A light flashed under the H-Pad 11's carriage. "There is a spy lock-down filter somewhere there . . ."

Alice shot through the door at high speed. "Mice deployed . . . rats ensnared . . ."

She stopped inches from the H-Pad 11.

"Oh! You!"

"I have been upcycled," muttered the H-Pad 11 as Hilda's voice rang through the room with a view and beyond . . .

"*Yes, yes—yeehaw!*"

"Switch that off," snapped Operator One.

"I can't," said the H-Pad 11.

A hand protruded from Alice's side.

"Alice to the rescue," she said with a ceremonial tickling of the H-Pad 11's undercarriage, and the H-Pad 11 hiccupped, belched, and spluttered . . .

"*Yes . . . yeeees . . . yeeeeees . . . oooooh . . . my . . .*"

Silence . . .

The Operators looked from one to the other with looks of relief.

"Perhaps a beverage," muttered Deidre.

A few nodded.

"Stand at ease," said a voice from nowhere.

"Oh for pickle sake, what is it now?" snapped Operator One.

The H-Pad 11 turned to Alice.

"It wasn't from me," snapped Alice.

Chapter Thirteen

HOT CHOCOLATE

"Fall seven times, stand up eight." —Japanese proverb " Fall seven times, get up six and sleep it off." —Ex-alcoholic

DBO's idea of saving the planet started with a planet run on clean energy from the hippie community.

Vegas, however, hadn't even thought that far. All she thought about was when could she use her drill again and how best to get back in contact with Hilda without it leading to a full-blown lecture, or worse, a pay cut.

DBO began to talk of connecting wind energy from the scarecrows and harnessing it from the water to all in the café. Vegas nodded, acting as if she understood; in truth, she felt like an idiot, all this *clean-energy malarkey* was the last thing on her mind.

She looked at DBO as her thin arms gestured with passion. Awe rose in Vegas like rising damp.

"Of course," said DBO, "your fish population is astounding. It could be what in the end saves our bacon."

"Bacon?" muttered the cook.

"She means 'planet'—it's an Earth phrase," said a voice from the back with inflated authority.

"Bacon, very droll," muttered Pot.

DBO, unperturbed, continued. She talked of the communists, the liberals, Karl Marx and where he went wrong. Then, to keep the robots happy, robot suffragettes, and in remembrance to her footman, how footmen too had their place.

"I always had a fondness for a footman," muttered a voice from the back.

"Me too, but I wouldn't want to eat one," laughed another.

A few chuckled; the waitress, convinced DBO was onto something, egged her on.

"Yes, carry on," said the robot, "tell us about this Earth."

"Earth—who wants to hear about them?" muttered a server, packing up. "And my shift's finished, I should be home, feet up, tucking into a hemp biscuit, not listening to this humanist claptrap."

"Perhaps we should retreat to the veranda," said Pope.

"Yes, Pope's right, we should go," said Prudence. She stood up.

DBO looked about; she needed to inspire. She talked of Maggie Thatcher, kindergartens, Germaine Greer burning her bra, and Armstrong walking on the moon.

"And did they give up," she said, "turn their backs, put their feet up?"

"Some might have wished they had," muttered Pope.

"Let her speak," muttered the waitress, who was won over by the fish compliment.

"When fate comes knocking on your door, what do you do—slam it shut or invite it in?" Said DBO, she jumped up on the table like Billy Graham on a roll. "We have a chance, we should grab it with both H-Pads."

"H-Pads?" muttered a voice from the back.

"She means hands," snapped the waitress.

Awe for this upstart was bursting upwards in Vegas like mercury in a heat wave.

DBO's mind was as sharp as an H-Pad, as quick as a man spy, and as easy to understand as any of Hilda's moods. In fact, her ability to think out of the box in a completely practical way was beyond anything Hilda had ever dreamt up.

Was she Messiah material?

Vegas thought of Hilda's plans, the Voted Ins on stationaries, the shed explosion, and that maniac laugh. The planet was on a collision course to nowhere, and Hilda laughed like a hyena on helium.

She had to contain herself, keep her dignity, her status . . . she mustn't let on that she hadn't a clue. *Act cool, for pickle's sake!*

DBO stretched out Verruca's plan on a table. The waitress raced to place empty mugs on each corner (for any curling of the edges) as an Alterationist, with a "here you go, luv," pulled a pen from behind her ear.

"It's all about timing, Hilda's 'holiday,'" said DBO.

Vegas stopped. *Hilda was on a holiday?*

DBO gestured, pointed, and delegated; the women nodded, suggested, and agreed, while Vegas struggled to follow. She was lost, confused. Hilda taking a holiday was as predictable as, well, the Voted In knowing about wind energy.

She looked at DBO in a new light. She knew so much . . . she even talked of a utopia. Was she in fact the new Messiah?

"You need to set the connections up before we can get the Operators in the room with a view to sort the paperwork."

"What paperwork?" said the authoritative voice at the back.

"We are about to perform a coup and you're talking of paperwork?" said Pot, attempting an equally authoritative voice.

She looked from one face to another like John the Baptist about to baptise. "By the time Hilda finds out, it would all be too late. We'll be in the room with a view, the city rebooted, and she will be on a permanent holiday."

Vega jumped up and punched the air with a loud "Yes!"

The others looked at her.

Vegas, red-faced, shuffled back into her seat.

"I've heard enough," muttered a disbeliever. "I'm heading for the library."

"They are stock-taking," shouted the voice from the back.

"Oh, how about the lounge?"

"Wait," said the waitress.

"We should listen," said another.

"Who cares?" said the disbeliever.

"This is an open-book establishment," said an Alterationist. "And to keep it that way, we need to listen."

Vegas stared down at her mug. *Perhaps I should lay off this stuff for a while.*

"Maybe this will help," said DBO. She flicked through her H-Pad, and the room with a view flashed onto her screen. The women gathered around to see the screen as the room with a view in all its opulent glory appeared in panoramic 3-D vision.

The women gasped.

Look at the size of that chandelier . . .

Size? It's shaped like a penis.

And the table—you could build a veranda on that . . .

A kitchen . . .

Shocking . . . absolutely shocking . . .

Vegas, squirming uncomfortably, said nothing as the women, along with the cleaning robot, united.

"This is outrageous," said the voice from the back.

"We are all equal," said the waitress.

"Yes, we're all equal," said the voice from the back.

"Equal? Pfff," said the cleaning robot.

DBO talked of the exploding shed, ending with her ever-exaggerated *capow!*

The women applauded, even the disbeliever.

"If I can do that, imagine what we can do," said DBO.

The women cheered.

"We can change things," shouted DBO.

"*Hear, hear!*"

"We can do something about this inequality."

"*Right on, sister!*"

"It's in our hands," said DBO. "Are you with me?"

"*Yes! Yes! Yes!*" The women applauded, this time like DBO was the new Messiah.

Chapter Fourteen

CAMPING

"Camping is as glamorous as cleaning the oven." –Bunnie

Don, Archie, and Legless were camped under the full glare of a streetlight and, thanks to the streetlight, Legless spent the night listening to the snores of Don and Archie.

While the others rumbled and snored, Legless pondered and grumbled. The time for interesting had passed. Funny stories, romantic songs—they were no longer *his* repertoire, and as for philosophical musings, they were completely out the window. He was entering his dark phase, which, opposed to his blue period, was fueled by anger, mostly directed at Beryl.

He rummaged for something to write with. He preferred paper, but as it was dark, that was out of the question. He switched on his phone; nothing . . . he headed to find the young ones. Maybe he could use their phone.

He slid into Woody's tent, spied his Nokia, muttered an out-of-date "rubbish" curse, then headed for the only other place he could think of; Bunnie's tent. He pulled a few screwed napkins from Bunnie's bag, a gran's hemp notepad from H2's backpack, and a box of Maltesers scrunched in Mex's hand and, with an eyebrow pencil, began to write. His wrinkled face lit up with inspiration as years spent banished on

Earth festered in his bowels. He didn't stop until the sun came up; he had the beginnings of a story worth reading.

On Earth, she would be described as a "has-been"—and on Planet Hy Man, she was just that, tall but stooped, with heels as high as her out-dated beehive hair.

And when the others started to make waking-up noises, he left.

Eunice and Patsy were in the kitchen, Eunice cooking and Patsy finishing a coffee.

Under Eunice's insistence, Patsy had shoved the wiry thing, along with its box, into the bin. Now it was buzzing like a personal alarm and Patsy couldn't take her eyes off it.

Eunice, tossing peels into the compost bucket, looked at her partner in disappointment.

"Why don't you stop looking at the bin and feed the dog?" she said.

Patsy filled Izzie's "just visiting" dog bowl with last night's chicken. Izzie licked her lips, made to move, then stopped . . .

"Go on, eat your dinner," said Patsy.

Izzie whimpered. Her bowl was sitting by the bin.

Patsy stared at the bin. The wiry thing had started to pulsate red, yellow, and green, lighting up the plastic bin like a neon sign.

"Come on, get your food," said Patsy.

Izzie shivered.

Patsy turned to Eunice. "I wonder if that thing in the bin is trying to tell us something?" She looked at Izzie. "Dogs usually have a sixth sense about these things."

"Just move the bowl," said Eunice.

Patsy moved Izzie's dish to the other side of the room. Izzie charged across to her bowl and began to gulp and belch at the same time.

"Did you feed her chicken?" said Eunice.

"Well, yes, isn't that what you said?"

Izzie licked her plate clean, looked up, and coughed up a small bone.

"No, she'll have the runs now," said Eunice, ripping skin off an onion.

Izzie squeaked a fart.

Eunice thrust a knife into the peeled onion and let out a "now look what you've done" tut.

Izzie began to bark at the bin.

"I mean it's flashing like an ambulance—do you think we should do something?" said Patsy.

"Like what?" Eunice huffed.

She tutted.

Patsy never listened, always jumped in, and now thanks to her *jumping in* their kitchen bin was lighting up like something from Chernobyl, and her with her hormones just sorted.

"Told you," she said, chopping with vengeance. "Didn't I say not to touch that thing? Now look at it, flashing like a Christmas tree. Probably radioactive and full of God knows what chemicals and we're soaking it all up. No wonder Izzie's farting."

"Aren't *we* being just a tad overdramatic," muttered Patsy.

"Dramatic? My ovaries are probably fucked by now," said Eunice.

"Ovaries? Since when have you wanted kids?" said Patsy.

"Don't have a choice now." Eunice sighed. "My eggs will be shriveled like . . . that dried tomato over there. And don't get me started on my thyroid."

Izzie coughed up a small piece of chicken; Patsy jumped to clean it up. "Thyroid—what's that got to do with our bin?"

Eunice turned to Patsy with a glare.

"My thyroid, as you know, is hanging on a cliff's edge—one whiff of Chernobyl over there and it'll have packed up for good."

"Packed up? What for, a holiday?" said Patsy, shoving Izzie outside.

"I'll be the side of a house by lunchtime," sniffed Eunice. "And what's that going to do to my mood?" She dumped the diced veg into a pot. "I'll end up back on those friggin' antidepressants—yet again."

"Would that be such a bad thing?" muttered Patsy.

"No need to be so flippant. Everything's a joke to you," said Eunice.

"Someone needs to lighten things up. You're like a badly written soap opera."

"That's right, blame it all on me." Eunice pointed to Patsy with her knife. "This is your fault, you know. You're the one who went and opened a can of friggin' cat food—honestly."

"Cat food? Don't you mean worms?" Patsy laughed.

"See, my hormones are making me all fussy-headed already. Next I'll be as dry as that dog food bowl over there."

Izzie trumpeted a loud fart.

"And you can get that farting machine out of here before it turns my cheese sauce."

Eunice said nothing. Once Patsy mentioned fuzzy-headed, there was no stopping her—she could argue longer than a drunk at closing time. She slid the so-called "radioactive ovarian destroyer" into her pocket, pulled Izzie's lead from the door handle, and, with an "I'm taking her for a walk," headed over to Bunnie's. Perhaps she could find some answers there.

Chapter Fifteen

EUNICE

"Bunnie: a woman with ridiculous necklaces, makeup that gives a clown a bad name, and toasted cheese to die for." –The H-Pad 11's description app

unnie woke up in her tent and looked across at Beryl and Mex. They were both snoring. She huffed; some sort of adventure this turned out to be. Johnny, her Johnny, was not Johnny after all. Instead, *he* was this so-called *Legless*, a twat in an outdated threadbare kilt that couldn't wipe a tear, let alone a nose, and a pony-tail that flopped about his head like a wet sock.

Some legend . . .

Bunnie had always called herself a people person, a woman who read people like recipes. Now it seemed there were people who read like a bleeding Chaucer poem, double meanings all over the place—impossible to understand.

She had had enough . . .

"I am going home," she shouted to Don.

"What?"

"I said I am going home to my Izzie."

Don sighed. "Thought you would."

❄

Mex's eyes fluttered open as she listened to Bunnie and Don; not the best thing to do when hungover.

So this is what it's all about, she thought. *The hard work, the hanging around Earth—to help some old git? To be bossed about by an Operator? Assisted by a robot who has hot flashes at the mere whiff of a hot chocolate—or worse, Woody?* She sighed. *A man spy was meant for grander things than this.*

"If you're going home, then so am I," shouted Mex with no idea how she was going to manage it.

"Aye, very good," muttered Bunnie.

Don thought about Bunnie. If she went home, what then? Would he ever make it to her bedroom?

He thought about the Identity meetings. Imagine Bunnie at one of those, with him dancing. That would get him into the bedroom and into her heart. He sighed. He hadn't danced for years, but an Identity never loses it.

He looked about his tent; it was a bit eggy for his liking. Archie was still snoozing, mumbling something about turning right and bus lanes, and Legless, the producer of the eggy smell, had disappeared, along with his things.

Don opened the tent flap for fresh air.

Where was that old boy off to now?

He tuned in to Legless's mind . . .

I've a story worth telling, I just need to learn how.

Don smiled. Legless was as easy to read as the *Daily Record*; he knew where Legless was going. There was only one place to learn, and it was in Edinburgh.

Don nudged Archie. "We need to go," he said. "Bunnie's making going-home noises, and I have an idea."

Archie grumbled, "About what, exactly, and why me? Not as if we get along."

"We can help each other," said Don.

Archie sat up. He wanted a coffee, a roll, a sausage, and a shower. He sniffed, scratched various bits of his hips, and eyed his opponent.

Don had caused a split in the Identities, many losing faith; now he wanted his help?

As if . . .

"Why should I help you when all you have done is cause problems?"

"I just question things, that's all," said Don.

"Question? You talked of new songs, and stories," said Archie.

"Nothing wrong with new."

"New? You chucked the whole Legless mantra out like last night's beer."

"I never mentioned beer."

"You took it too far."

"You don't move with the times," said Don.

"Yeah, well, sometimes those so-called *times* are just not worth following," huffed Archie.

Don looked at Archie. "But you still want the Identities to follow the old ways, don't you?"

Archie sighed. "Aye, well, that's not gonna happen now, is it? Not with that dickhead Legless. If anything he'll close the whole Identity community down. Not like he lives up to his legend, is it?"

"There's a link missing," said Don.

"Link? What the planetary hell are you on about?"

"Did you not see him give Beryl what for?"

"Well, yes," said Archie.

"He was funny, inspiring, the anger burned in his storytelling friggin' soul—*she*'s the missing link."

Archie looked unconvinced.

"She puts fire in his belly—pep in his step."

Archie said nothing.

"Sperm in his balls."

Archie pulled a face.

"And we can train him."

"Train him? That man is as trainable as a stick insect."

Don talked of how the Identities felt rootless.

Archie said nothing.

Don talked of the Identities meeting their father, including Archie.

Archie shrugged.

"Maybe bond?"

Archie sighed.

"Like the old days?" said Don. "Isn't that what you want?"

"The past is the past," muttered Archie.

"He's gone to the Storytelling Center," Don finally added.

Archie stopped. "The Storytelling Center here in Edinburgh?"

Don nodded.

"Why didn't you say so in the first place, instead of all that sperm talk?"

"I only mentioned it once," muttered Don.

"That place is legendary," said Archie. "Not only the best cakes *and* dance floor, but they train storytellers—even idiots like Legless."

Archie, revitalized with new hope, attempted to jump out of his sleeping bag.

"First things first," he said, struggling with his zipper. "Coffee, and a hot roll."

He rolled over and crashed into the wall of the tent. "You up, girls? We're heading out."

"What?" shouted Bunnie.

Archie, still struggling with his zipper, grunted, "Come on, women, there's rolls to be eaten and coffee to sip."

"Aren't we going home?" shouted Bunnie.

"Aye, in good time," said Archie as DJ appeared and slid Archie's zipper like it was greased with oil.

Archie stepped out of his sleeping bag to reveal old-fashioned drawstring pajamas gaping open about his groin. DJ and Don watched as he began wrestling his sleeping bag into its holder.

"Could you not have worn pull-on PJs like everyone else?" muttered Don.

Archie stopped, the gape—now as wide as a tent door—revealing a manhood best kept for candlelight. The sleeping bag oozed from its bag.

"I like a bit of fresh air about things," muttered Archie.

"Mate, that is obvious, but no one else wants to see it," said DJ.

Bunnie appeared at the door. "What do you mean all in good time . . . Jesus." She averted her eyes.

"Don't you ever knock?" snapped Archie.

"Have you not heard of pull-ons?" snapped Bunnie.

"We're off to the Storytelling Center," Don said to Bunnie.

"Thought you said we were heading home," said Bunnie.

"It's on the way," said Archie, vainly trying to keep his pajamas closed while squashing the sleeping bag into its bag.

"Heard that before," said Bunnie, snatching the sleeping bag from Archie.

The three men watched as the sleeping bag submitted to every push and prod and within seconds was packed into a neat ball in its bag.

Bunnie pulled the drawstring tight with a decisive knot.

"And someone needs to mind Beryl," said Don.

Bunnie glared at the three men.

"Keep her from wandering off."

Bunnie thrust the bag at a sheepish Archie. "If you think I'm babysitting that woman for some male bonding bollocks, you can think again."

DJ, like many Identities before him, often felt not only that Star Trek was more laughable than not, but that he was better suited to such fantasies than Earth itself. Some Identities suggested the answers were in the past with a father who had left without even a "my son," and for the first time in his life, DJ agreed.

He wanted to let Legless know what it was like to be left. He wanted remorse from Legless. And as Bunnie pushed into submission the remaining sleeping bags, DJ knew Beryl would be just the sort to help.

"I'll mind her," he said.

"Good man," said Don, tossing a sleeping bag into the back of the car.

Archie slapped him on the shoulder. "The whole Identity community is depending on you," he said, sending Bunnie into a series of tutting.

Chapter Sixteen

PATSY

"All great things start with something simple." —Inventor of the H-Pad

Woody woke to find Pete's warm, padded, Teflon face snuggled next to his and sighed. It felt nice. He looked across to see H2 cross-legged, peering into her H-Pad, nodding.

"Who are you talking to?" he said.

"DBO," she said with relief.

"DBO?"

"Yes, and she says we have to move before Beryl finds out."

"Oh, I see."

DBO gestured to her H-Pad.

"There's a component missing. H2 knows where it is."

"Component?" said Woody.

"Yes, a wiry thing, should click in here."

Woody nodded.

"Once clicked, telespraying will be a breeze."

"Telespraying?" said Woody.

"Think Star Trek transporter," Pete muttered into his pillow.

Woody's face lit up. "A transporter? Are you for real?"

"Yes, how else did you think we got here?" said H2.

"A transporter like in Star Trek?"

"It's *telespray*, and unlike Star Trek, it is silent."

"That's how you move about?" said Woody.

"Well, not all the time. Just for planets and things," said H2.

"Unbelievable," he muttered.

"It's not exactly rocket science," said H2.

"Can't believe it," said Woody. "Does it hurt?"

"Only when you land in a disabled john," muttered Pete.

"By the way," said H2, "do you know what a coup is?"

"You want a car as well?" said Woody.

"A sudden, violent, illegal takeover of power," muttered Pete. He sat up and smiled at his pal. Woody smiled back . . .

"Oh," muttered H2. "Maybe it means something different on Planet Hy Man."

As the group congregated outside their tents with rolls from the breakfast van, Beryl looked about. She wondered where Legless was but didn't like to look like she cared. Instead, she nibbled at her roll with great intensity.

"We've got him covered," said Archie.

"What?" said Beryl.

"Legless. He won't go far, will he, DJ?"

"Oh, I see," said Beryl. "Like I care. I mean it's not as if he can save the planet or anything." She looked about. "Is it?"

"Talking of saving the planet," said Woody.

"What?" muttered Beryl.

"We must follow a lead," said Woody.

"Without you," said H2.

Beryl brushed a fly from her face and stared into the distance.

"Ma'am," said Pete, "it's vital that we split."

Beryl didn't hear; she was still thinking of all that Legless had said and trying to deal with the feeling of shame inside her.

"Split?" she muttered.

"Best you come with us," said DJ.

"With you?" said Beryl.

"Yes," said DJ.

"We are off home. Aren't we, Don?" said Bunnie.

"In a manner of speaking," said Don.

All in good time, ESP-ed DJ with a look at Beryl.

Beryl blinked. "I see," she muttered, unaware that her steel-trap mind had finally been prized open.

While Patsy was waiting for her hormones to settle, Eunice was exploring Bunnie's porch and beyond. Once she started, she couldn't stop. Moving from the porch to the inside, she opened cupboards and peered where she shouldn't, learning little except that Bunnie liked her drawers tidy, anything that was pink or orange, lace underwear that "locked things into place," and bras with underwire that could hold a tent in a storm. She also, like many women, had a thing for shoes that were impossible to wear but looked sexy on a shelf.

Patsy, a sporty, DIY, flat-shoes sort of woman, gazed upon a wall lined with shoes hidden behind a white curtain. She picked up a platform shoe of glittering pink and burnt orange and thought of Eunice.

In her day, Eunice would have worn this to the co-op, thought Patsy. *Now it's all about hormones.*

She slid the shoe on and was just about to explore her look in the mirror when the wiring thing pulsated in her breast pocket. Soon it was making noises like a hearing aid that wasn't properly fitted.

She took it out, jiggled it, shook it, and finally, with a good bash, realized that H2, Pete, Woody, and Mex were standing behind her.

H2, Pete, and Woody had made a beeline for Bunnie's house; according to DBO, they hadn't much time. Mex, feeling delicate, was happy to follow anything to get away from Beryl and the whole Legless thing. She dozed on the empty bus as H2, armed with Beryl's H-Pad, talked to another female voice about Hilda's holiday and a drill, her chatter lulling Mex to sleep . . .

She dreamed of drills and food, of Izzie and Beryl fighting over a roll and a sausage while Don bent over a drill and talked of men in white coats. By the time they reached Bunnie's house, Mex had, to quote Bunnie, been to hell and back.

How I miss my home, she thought. *The smell of the market, the footmen snoozing on their feet jolting awake at the falling moment and my pad. To run my hands along the gold doors, stare through the glass, and catch Pete off guard, reading something he shouldn't—*

"I want to go home," she muttered.

No one noticed.

The lights were on in Bunnie's house and the door was ajar.

They walked in, unsure of what to do. The last thing they expected to see was Patsy, posed like a drag queen's first time in heels, talking to Izzie.

Patsy, a muscular woman standing like a workman in seventies Elton John platform shoes, looked anything but intimidating. One step and she was heading for the floor!

H2 rose to the occasion. "Who are you?"

Patsy held her ground with a stare. She was not an easy woman to shame. After all, she had a right to be here; she was dog-sitting. She was Bunnie's pal. She had even drunk this place dry on a few occasions . . .

"Who are you?" she said.

"I asked first," snapped H2.

The front door slammed.

Patsy started and overbalanced.

Izzie jumped into Mex's arms.

Patsy righted herself as familiar footsteps trotted down the hallway.

Shit, thought Patsy.

The door creaked open and Eunice appeared.

"Shit," muttered Patsy.

"What the hell is going on here?" Said Eunice, then, spotting Izzie, snapped, "Give her to me."

Mex clutched tighter.

Izzie squeaked a fart.

The H-Pad lit up. Verruca, with a small cough, interrupted.

Patsy and Eunice turned to the H-Pad.

"What the fuck was that?" they said.

Chapter Seventeen

THE STORYTELLING CENTER

"The purpose of a wiry thing is hard to define without a name." – H2

Eunice, a woman convinced her hormones were radioactive, had no time for small talk. If Patsy was holding her ground, Eunice was digging the trench. She knew when there was a serious threat to her home, and with Patsy out of action on Elton John shoes, it was up to her to take control.

"I want you lot out now or I'm calling the police," she huffed. "And give me that dog."

Mex shook her head.

"Right, that's it, I am calling the police."

"Look, the dog is irrelevant," said H2. "All I need is that wiry thing."

"This?" said Patsy, pulling the wiry thing from her pocket.

Izzie whimpered.

"Why should I give it to you?"

"Do you know what that is?" said H2.

Izzie eyed the wiring thing pulsating in Patsy's hands, then cringed into Mex.

"There, there, poppet," muttered Mex.

"It slips in here," she said, gesturing to the H-Pad. "Some would call it a tracker."

"Or a component," said Woody.

Eunice pulled a face. "That is a component?"

"In a fashion," muttered Pete.

"Doesn't look like a component, doesn't act like one—"

"Here we go," muttered Patsy.

"—it's more nuclear," said Eunice.

"Don't be insulting," snapped H2. "The last thing that thing is is nuclear."

"Try telling that to my ovaries."

"Will you forget about your ovaries," said Patsy.

Without listening, Eunice continued, "I mean look at it. It's lit up like a power station. If that thing isn't nuclear, then Elton John over there is a stripagram."

"Oh. Ha-ha," muttered Patsy.

Woody tutted. "Nuclear doesn't exist where they come from."

"Where is that then, the Milky Way?"

"Close," muttered H2.

Mex, up to this point, was a man spy coasting along with things. Sure, she had had her fun, enjoyed a few drinks, had a few laughs, hung out with men dressed as women. But that was then and this was now. Something was up and she had to focus. The conversations on the bus filtered back to her; the word *telespraying* lingered. Then it hit her right as Eunice mentioned "Milky Way"—*they were going home.* She hugged Izzie. Soon she would be a man spy again with all her strength and senses and without Beryl and Hilda on holiday. Life would be a breeze.

"You can come too, poppet," she muttered to Izzie.

She decided that it was time for action—kicking action, her calling card. She, with her eye on the wiry thing, made for a simple "knock an object from the hands" kick. One she had done many times on Planet Hy Man, but never on Earth.

Patsy saw it coming and, forgetting her "weighs a ton" platform shoes, made a dive. It was like she was superglued to the ground.

Both women crashed to the floor, along with Izzie.

The wiry thing bounced from Patsy's hands, across the tiles, towards Eunice's feet.

Izzie yelped, then, realizing the love of her life may be in danger, made a heroic dive, leading to a belch, followed by a gulp and a "what have I done" whimper.

The component disappeared.

"Shit!" muttered most in the room.

"Now look what you've done—made Izzie a nuclear carrier pigeon," said Eunice.

And before someone could correct Eunice with "dog," Verruca's voice bellowed from the H-Pad . . .

"Group hug—with the dog, when you're ready."

Mex grabbed the H-Pad, slapped it against Izzie's chest, and nodded for the others to join, and without thinking, Woody jumped in.

Piff poff puff . . . boom!

The room was empty except for Patsy and Eunice.

Legless made his way to the Storytelling Center, a man hell-bent on finishing his story. In fact, so emotional was he that he was completely unaware of Archie and Don reading his mind.

When he walked into the Storytelling Center, the manager clocked him straightaway and pulled what he thought was a homeless person aside.

"Can I help you?" he said.

"I have stories to complete," said Legless. "Plus, I think I am a bit early."

The manager, with no interest in what Legless meant by "early," nodded a sympathetic "okay," pointing him to an out-of-the-way corner.

"How about you sit over here, with some soup?"

Legless's face lit up. "Soup? That would hit the spot."

Legless nestled into the corner and pulled a ball of paper from his pocket; the Malteser's packet fluttered to the floor along with the eyebrow pencil. The manager watched as Legless pressed the balled paper flat, licked the eyebrow pencil, and began to scribble.

When the pencil broke, the manager could take no more.

"Here," he said, "some pen and paper for that story, and some bread for your soup."

Chapter Eighteen

EDINBURGH

"There was a time when men in white coats took away the delusional to give 'em drugs that caused dribbling. Not anymore; the only white coats you see now is on washing machine adds." – Don explaining One Flew Over the Cuckoo's Nest to Pete

The Edinburgh Festival was a tricky place for Identities; finding unhappy women was not easy, and making contact with all the energetic distractions required an expertise not all Identities had—apart from the Storytelling Center. It was the new Mecca for Identities, and as Legless looked around, he understood why.

Legless had never been. The idea of humans telling stories seemed laughable to him, and yet here he was in a café with a warm wooden floor perfect for dancing and sitting on handmade wooden furniture excellent for storytelling. A place full of books about legends, fairies, witches, and warriors. A place full of story lovers curious of the old traditions—just the sort easy to connect with.

Why had he waited so long?

Legless made use of being early and spent the day ESP-ing along with writing his stories. Although his "recruiting women ESP" was rusty, he was a man on a mission. He needed an audience, the bigger the better to humiliate Beryl with. Soon he had made eye contact with some of the staff and, buoyed on by his success, moved on to the customers.

His first was an easy target, a young student still not at home in

Edinburgh. Her loneliness oozed from every thought as she pondered the history of Bonnie Prince Charlie on a bookshelf.

As she idly wondered how she was to fill the rest of the day, let alone that night, Legless caught her eye.

She blinked, took the book to the cashier, and sighed as the cashier, with a smile, slid the book in a bag, along with instructions on "how to get to where you are coming tonight."

Legless watched another woman, her children racing about like mini banshees. He caught her eye; she blinked.

Yes, she thought, *my mum will mind the kids. I can come.*

He smiled at her. She smiled as her mini banshee produced a book and placed it on the counter.

Legless took his empty soup bowl to the counter. A young chap took it and, with a nod, thought, *Don't worry, I have the stage set.*

Legless, with a beguiling wink he hadn't used in years, sashayed back to his seat with a coffee—extra cream, a dash of chocolate, and a chocolate-covered coffee bean melting on the saucer. He slipped the bean onto his tongue and began to ESP Identities within reach.

He was going to tell the full Beryl story and impress the Identities. *The timing was perfect.*

When he heard from his first Identity, he was ecstatic; he had no idea if his plan would work, but as one connected, so did another and another, all with mixed feelings of curiosity, anger, and excitement. Legless, their father, had vanished, and for the first time in their lives, they could find out why and maybe give him "what for" as well.

The energy from the Identities filled Legless. He had been out of the game for so long he had forgotten about comradeship, friendship, and joshing. Now, as he sat staring at the chocolate rim of his empty coffee cup, he wondered about tonight. After all the stories, would there be some joshing?

He ran his finger around the rim and licked it. Would they be interested in what he had to say? Will they understand his story or just see him as a man outsmarted by Beryl?

The fear of the unknown excited him. That and revenge . . .

The manager had no idea what was going on, except that as time went on, the homeless man was looking less like a homeless man and more like a good old-fashioned storyteller. He watched as Legless waltzed up to the counter, sometimes for a napkin, other times with an empty plate from another table. Most women gazed as he swayed past, no longer an invisible old man but a man of intrigue and a beguiling wink. A man who sauntered with a swish of a kilt, whose tiny arse swayed with the seduction of a Jamaican stripteaser.

And Legless looked as comfortable with every glance, as any self-respecting Jamaican stripper would.

"This book," he said to a traveler, "is not the best. Try this one."

Soon others were asking him about books, and as he talked of the past, they listened, eager for more. Even the manager listened. And when the center finally closed, no one noticed when Legless stayed behind.

Bunnie, under the impression that they were heading home, took a paternal view to Beryl, a woman dazed with guilt. She steered her to the car and packed her into the back.

"Never thought about it before," said Beryl. "It's not easy being in charge, thinking of everyone. Perhaps I wasn't so right after all." She looked at Bunnie. "What if I was completely wrong?"

Bunnie patted her on the hand and slid a coffee into it.

"Drink your coffee, you'll feel better."

"But what if it was all my fault and Hilda was right? If someone like her is right, what does that make me?"

"Come on, luv, let's get you home."

We're not going home just yet, ESP-ed Archie to Bunnie, *and you're fine with that.*

Bunnie, blinking, said, "Oh."

She piled their bags into the boot and slid into the car beside Beryl.

DJ slid in on the other side of Beryl.

Don drove and Archie directed. He knew Edinburgh and its secret parking places like no one else. He had also made contact with the others.

It was nighttime when they arrived at the Storytelling Center, and it was closed.

Beryl was about to say "What are we doing here?" when she stopped. She could recognize that chatter of voices anywhere. *Just like the room with a view.*

Chapter Nineteen

ENCORE

"Happy women are as receptive to ESP-ing as a teenager is to a parent's advice." —A frustrated Identity

They stood at the front door. To a passerby, it looked dark and shut. Archie muttered, "Encore."

A hand slid from the door and grabbed his collar. Archie, with a "do the same" look at the others, disappeared.

Bunnie followed; she muttered "encore" and pushed Beryl to the door, and Beryl with a "really" was pulled in. Don, DJ, and Bunnie followed to find Beryl adjusting her beehive with a ruffled "was that necessary" tut.

The bookshop was lit with candles and smelt of vanilla; in the shadows concealing the café beyond hung a tatty purple curtain with gold stars painted on it. From the floors above could be heard the faint murmur of a Scottish accent . . .

"And now let's hear one of Jimmy Shand's favorites—the two-step," followed by a chord pressed on an accordion . . .

Deeeeeeeee de de de dill-de dill-de de de dill-de dill-de . . .

Before Beryl had time to moan about the noise or Bunnie explain who Jimmy Shand was, a gnarled mechanical hand appeared from behind the till. It was attached to the counter with a contractible brace and moved like a crane. With a "you first" gesture to Archie, it beckoned, and Archie threw himself into a starfish pose. The hand patted him down, pulled his phone from his pocket, and tossed it like a coin across the room into a bag hanging on the wall.

Beryl looked at Bunnie. "And is *that* absolutely necessary?"

The hand motioned to Beryl.

She glared at the yellowed, stained fingers covered in rings and jumped away.

"Assume the star position," said Bunnie with a push.

Piff poff puff . . . boom!

Izzie appeared, inches from Eunice.

Izzie blinked, jumped into Eunice's arms, and licked her face. Patsy fingered the collar around her neck. She pulled out a note tucked into it.

Component removed—no harm done . . .

The men were ushered through the purple "star" curtain into the café lit by hundreds of tea lights laid across the floor, and Identities in various stages of undress, changing into their kilts.

DJ and Archie knew the drill. Don, a bit rusty, followed. First, they picked their way through the sea of candles on the floor—a sort of limbering-up, tippy-toe exercise in preparation for "light on your feet" dancing—then, they rummaged through the pile of kilts in the corner, holding the kilts against each other to see which would fit.

The other Identities didn't notice; they were revved up high on thoughts of Legless. Over the years, Identities had yearned to see their father, waiting for a special bonding moment, a son-and-father moment about women, Earth, and why they felt as out of place as a paper cup in a china shop. Some still waited, while others had given up and talked of Legless as if he was just a story, a legend as real as the tooth fairy.

Now, *out of the blue*, the "tooth fairy" was here, and the excitement was fever pitch. They talked and joked, occasionally peering up and down the stairs, wondering when he was to appear.

As they did, DJ, Don, and Archie listened to the Identities joshing, ESP style . . . a style, it seemed, free of any inhibitions.

I heard he's old, aged, thin.

Wouldn't you be after all that shagging?

Tell me about it.

The whole world and its dog will see him tonight, the first in years.

Yeah, and what's his friggin' excuse?

DJ, clutching an itchy-looking kilt, followed Don and Archie into the gents', planning a quick ESP in private. The gents', however, was full, two Identities in a cubical adjusting each other's kilts and three by the urinals jostling, swapping kilts, and moaning about how useless the changing facilities were.

There was a time when changing was all part of the adventure; now there's not even a mirror.

Not even room to swing a kilt.

The loo roll holder crashed to the floor. *Oops, sorry . . .*

The other identity, with an unimpressed glare, rubbed his backside . . .

Sorry? That was my arse, you wanker.

The identity glared at each, which, thanks to the size of the cubicle, meant nose to nose.

Better your arse than other things . . .

Ha-ha, very funny—what are you, a comedian?

One of the Identities by the urinals stopped, his kilt sorted. He eyed the two in the cubicle.

Focus!

The two glared back at him.

In a john?

DJ, Don, and Archie said nothing; they were experts at blanking their thoughts and were just about to head out when thoughts from somewhere outside the toilet ESP-ed to them.

Focus all you like, I am still going to spill the beans on this Beryl . . .

I can't wait, DJ ESP-ed.

Neither can I, son . . .

DJ looked at Don, with a "*Pfff* . . ."

Chapter Twenty

THE DRILL

"A drill never works alone." —Verruca's robot

The hand ushered Bunnie and Beryl behind the counter and through a heavy velvet curtain. Beryl stared at the thick walls and spiral stairs. Bunnie, with a "you first," pushed her on.

The stairway was lit by tea lights and filled with the noise of Scottish dance music and the fast chatter of women. Some would have found it mystical; Beryl, however, stumbling in the dark, spent her time choking on the incense with as much noise as possible. The scent of vanilla always made her feel sick.

She stumbled on the seventh step and let out a loud "Oh, for pickling *shit*!"

"Shhhh," snapped Bunnie.

"Nearly broke my ankle," muttered Beryl.

"No need to shout about it."

"Shout about it? You try walking in these heels in this—this nightmare-from-nowhere dungeon. I mean is all this cloak-and-dagger stuff *absolutely* necessary?"

"Do you have any romance in you at all?" hissed Bunnie.

"Romance?" tutted Beryl. "What in the name of sperm is that?"

Bunnie pulled a face as Beryl tripped again.

"Don't worry," said a young man's voice from above.

The two women turned to each other with a "where did that come from?" look.

"That step is spaced differently to the others," said the voice.

"What a sensible idea," snapped Beryl. "Especially in the dark."

"To trip up potential intruders—you're not the first."

"Well that *is* a relief, hate to have been the first," hissed Beryl.

Bunnie threw Beryl a "will you shut it" look as the curtain at the top of the stairs opened. Beryl staggered in, followed by Bunnie.

The room was lit with fairy lights and candles and was so smoky that Beryl began to do a fine impression of a dog gagging. She leant against the large fireplace waiting for a reaction. Bunnie, however, was busy eyeing up the hot chocolate nearby.

"Help yourself," said the young man's voice, "but mind, it is all soon starting."

Bunnie stared across the Victorian-looking chambers. The one in the distance looked like a sort of workshop. She sipped the hot chocolate, her mouth tingling with pleasure.

"Ahhh."

She sipped again and, with a louder "arrrrh," moved to investigate the workshop.

"You should try some," she said to Beryl.

"Can't," coughed Beryl. "Choking . . ."

"Better be quick," said the young man's voice. "Soon starting."

"I am choking . . ." Beryl let out a loud gag. "You can't hurry a throat-clearing."

"Up the stairs before it shuts," said the young man's voice.

Bunnie thrust the remains of her drink into Beryl's hands. "Skull this," she said and made for the stairs. Beryl skulled, gulped, and, with a "wait for me," followed.

As they reached the top of the stairs, a young head flashed from behind another velvet curtain.

"This way."

Bunnie and Beryl entered and, wiping chocolate from their lips, speechlessly stared . . .

In front of them was a large wood-paneled room with huge floorboards and a painted ceiling. It was full of women, some sitting cross-legged and others sprawled out on cushions like Greek goddesses. They were all ages, colors, and sizes: mothers and daughters, sisters and friends, chatting with excitement like something amazing was about to happen. Amongst the women were water-smoking pipes and trays of cakes—chocolate puffs filled with cream; cupcakes with so much brightly colored icing they could hardly stand; tray bakes covered in coconut, chocolate, or toffee; and tiny bite-sized sponges oozing cream with jam dripping down the side.

No one noticed Beryl and Bunnie, until Beryl's stomach trumpeted a loud rumble . . .

Grrrrrrr . . .

Silence.

The other women stared at Beryl's beehive.

Bunnie smiled a "hello."

Beryl muttered an "at ease."

A couple of women coughed . . . while another, stretched out like a lizard basking in the sun, sucked on her water pipe. She blew a ring of smoke, eyed the two, then, gesturing with her pipe, muttered, "A couple of cushions over there, honey."

Beryl, realizing that sitting on cushions required boots off, began a "standing on one leg while pulling the boot from the other" position and staggered.

Bunnie, after slipping her shoes off, caught sight of Beryl, now hopping like a lizard on hot sand, and moved to help. She tugged at the boot; it was wedged hard.

The other women watched like they had never seen the pulling-boot position before, let alone hopping on one foot . . .

Beryl grunted.

Bunnie pulled. "What, are these superglued on?"

"Just another tug," grunted Beryl.

Bunnie pulled, Beryl tugged . . . finally, with an over-the-top toe-pointing, Bunnie, with an almighty wrench, shouted "Gotcha" and staggered backwards into the wall behind.

Beryl crashed to the floor, knocking over a water pipe.

Water spilled onto the cushions.

The women gasped.

Beryl clamored to adjust the water pipe, spilling more water.

Bunnie, with a "friggin' hell," attempted a mopping-up with nearby napkins.

"You're not the first," soothed a young male voice. "Relax, it will dry . . ."

The other women, with a sigh of relief, broke into chatter again.

The cushions didn't make the rock-hard floor comfortable. Bunnie, trying to make the best of things, attempted a cross-legged pose, while Beryl grunted and groaned into several lounging poses, each more uncomfortable than the last.

"In the name of Hy Man, why don't they have some chairs?" snapped Beryl.

Bunnie hissed a "Shut it" as a few woman eyed the weird beehive gran.

"Here, suck on this, it makes it easier," said the lizard-lounging woman. She handed Beryl her water pipe.

Beryl sucked the sweet smoke into her lungs, and a strawberry taste hit her tongue. Without one cough or a splutter, she closed her eyes. Warm fudgy feelings seeped into her chest and her stomach, and if she knew what a hug was, she would have said that that was just how it felt. She sucked again, this time as long as possible.

"Pete would be comfortable here," she said, smirking.

"Give me that," snapped Bunnie. "The last thing we need is you happy." She looked at Beryl's lopsided grin. "Don't think I could stand it."

"Bring on the kilts," shouted one woman.

"Oooh, yes," shouted another.

The voice from nowhere laughed as the curtain opened to reveal a small platform with DJ at the microphone and his band squashed behind him. He waved to Beryl. Bunnie nudged her, and she waved back.

"We are live with Hamish on the accordion, me on spoons, and Nick on drums . . . let's put the Gay into Gordon," he shouted as the room filled with wolf-whistling.

Chapter Twenty-One

THE WARM-UP

"Warming up is not the same as cooling down, despite similar moves." –Pete's Yoga: An Android's Best Friend Volume 11

As DJ left to do, as he put it, "what he had to do," Don and Archie watched the younger Identities in the café warming up for their kilted entrance, some with stretches and yoga poses, others lunging or arabesque-ing their leg into the air. One round feller even attempted a headstand, landing in a half-moon pose with a laugh instead.

Focus, ESP-ed the Identity from the gents and then, remembering the voice, blushed.

Don and Archie had seen it all before. As they were older, less was expected of them. Acrobatics and leg-lifting was for the young; older Identities such as Don and Archie didn't even have to dance. Their role was more a cheering "come on, lads" sort of thing. Besides, they had mastered the art of pleasing women with listening, along with eye contact and the odd interesting story—why burst into a somersault when a "tell me about it" would do?

The women, tired of eating chocolate and cake, began stamping their feet . . .

We want kilts!

We want kilts!

They're getting restless, ESP-ed one.

Time for upstairs, ESP-ed another.

Don and Archie, without ESP-ing, looked at each other and with a "we need to focus" nod followed behind the others.

Identities entered with their kilts swinging about their behinds, showing just enough to make a woman forget her chocolate; it was as seductive as a six pack.

"It's time for some stripping," said DJ.

The women cheered and whistled as DJ began a spirited Gay Gordons.

"'Strip the Willow'!" he shouted as men of all shapes and sizes showed off their underwear like cancan dancers.

One look at an Identity's incognito underwear and the women went crazy, squealing with delight, egging the Identities on, and soon they were swinging their kilts so high that any feelings of "should I" and "who's looking" were forgotten.

Beryl had never seen dancing before, not even on BBC repeats. She, like the Voted In, had heard it caused blindness; now, here she was watching dancing with not even a hint of blurring.

"Don't you need glasses or something?" she said to Bunnie. "I mean isn't it bad for the eyes, all this twirling and pelvic thrusting?"

Don after a few small soft shoe taps, twirled about Bunnie. She laughed.

"Blind? Dancing?" She looked at Beryl. *The only thing you get from dancing is the wrong fella, the wrong song, and possibly heartburn.*

"Oh? Not blind then?"

"No! Staring at the sun will do it, poking your eye will do it, but dancing and wanking are pleasures that just make you puffed."

"Wanking?"

Bunnie looked at her. "I'll tell you later, honey."

Under the dimmed lights and smoky atmosphere, the Identity's underpants lit up with fairy lights, smiley faces, florescent pliable sticks, and expandable unmentionables. Bunnie cried with laughter; in all her years, she had never seen Don jump up and down, let alone dance, and here he was twirling like a stripper—amongst all those underpants.

Beryl was spellbound, captivated, by the magnificent underpants that were way better than the phallic chandelier in the room with a view. Soon she forgot about going blind; in fact, she forgot about everything, from her *shame* to *leadership*, from "how will I get out of here?" to "where is the next smoking water pipe?" She forgot it all, basking in the feelings staring at the Identity's hypnotic underpants gave her.

Bunnie cheered Don on, and he, getting into the swing of things, attempted a real man's cancan. The women clapped…

"On yer self."

"Och, the wee man."

"Higher, higher."

"Trip the light fantastic," yelled DJ. "The two-step, the three-step, and the five-and-a-half-step."

"The side-step, the back-step, and slide-your-leg-up-your-man-step," yelled the audience as Don staggered to a seat next to Bunnie.

The Identities began to pull women from their chairs as DJ's band moved on to a Canadian barn dance. It was danced nothing like Bunnie remembered from the weddings she'd been to. She watched the Identities dip and dive, occasionally running their fingers through their partners' hair. "I want that," she muttered and, with a tussle befitting a shampoo add, let down her hair like the others had.

Don watched. "Let me," he was about to whisper when Gary, an Identity with a reputation for "getting what he wanted faster than a chip pan fire," pulled Bunnie up from her chair. Gary, light on his feet, manipulated her into steps she had never dreamed of.

Ed, an Identity that most knew as "the joker," moved to Beryl. He dropped to his knees in a "will you marry me?" pose.

Beryl shook her head.

"Go on," shouted Bunny, and was about to add "You know you want to!" when Gary lifted her off her feet, swirled her around, and landed her tightly in his arms. He squeezed her hard; she gasped an "ouch" and looked for Don.

Ed placed his hand around Beryl's waist. She felt delicious—just how Legless used to make her feel—and for a moment, she wished she could let down her steel trap of a beehive. She looked into his eyes, her body hypnotized into a sense of wistful arousal. He eyed her hair, made to touch, and then went for a brush of her cheek with his. By the third turn, she was rubbing cheeks like a cat about the legs of its owner and giggling like a schoolgirl.

Legless heard it all. Hidden behind a thick velvet window curtain by the drinks trolley, he listened and waited. He had to get the timing right.

Chapter Twenty-Two

APPLAUSE AND MORE

"For such a small size, the prostate causes monumental problems." –Legless

Don pulled up a chair by Archie.

"I am not sure, but I think he's watching."

Archie took a sip of hot chocolate. He didn't hear. He was watching Bunnie dance with Gary, an Identity at the height of his hypnotic powers, a known mover. He was young and full of such talk as "use it or lose it," "having it all," and "believing in yourself"—the sort of claptrap which, as Archie put it, got many humans in trouble.

Gary, using his trademark fifties jitterbug move, twirled Bunnie from side to side. Bunnie's heart skipped a beat as he then whisked her into a frenzy of turns that had her hair flowing, her red skirt billowing, and her seeing double.

Gary went in for a whisper . . .

"Fancy a little dipping?"

Dipping?

Bunnie looked into his green eyes and was just about to tell him to stuff his dipping when Gary, hell-bent on impressing her, went for a tango move.

He grabbed her thigh. "Tango, ma'am?"

The Identities clapped and whistled as Bunnie, with a glare, wrestled her leg free.

"Tango? You've been tossing me about like a spinning top and now you want me to tango?"

The Identities stopped clapping.

"Did you see that?" muttered Archie. "He just broke every rule in the manual."

Don didn't answer; he'd disappeared.

Archie looked around. *What are you up to?*

Don, at the back of the room checking curtains, stopped. *I can sense him—he's here somewhere.*

Bunnie made to sit down.

Gary, assuming that Bunnie was sad, lonely, and not used to attention, pulled her up. He had no idea that she was strong, independent, and happy to prove it; he had no idea any woman could be.

So you like it slow then? he ESP-ed, pulling Bunnie closer with a seductive hum. *All women love a hum . . .*

Bunnie pulled away and sat down.

Gary pulled her up.

The Identities stopped. *Pulling up? Since when was that allowed?*

Identities, once engaged in women "baiting," often develop tunnel vision, continuing to persuade, but pulling up—that was never allowed. Pulling up is what got humans in trouble, well, that and not listening . . .

Gary looked into Bunnie's eyes and reached for her hair . . .

"Will ye go lassie go, and will we all go together all around the blooming heather, will ye go lassie go?"

"I'm not your lassie, fancy pants."

Gary didn't listen. He, like a *man* idiot, assumed "no" meant "playing hard to get."

He pulled her closer.

The Identities stared. One even tried to stop Gary with a *you've taken it too far* ESP.

Legless listened from behind the curtain. He had spent all his energy trying to keep his mind blank while listening for the right moment. Then he sensed Don close by.

What is he up to? Bollocks, shouldn't have thought that . . . or that. He sighed. This was the reason he stopped coming to these things . . . keeping your mind blank was near impossible.

Bunnie glared. "What the frig are you doing?"

"Making you happy," said Gary.

She looked at the young Identity, cocksure of himself. "Do you even know what would make me happy?"

Me? ESP-ed Gary.

Bunnie huffed. Where the hell was Don when you needed him?

Legless could hear the crowd hush, he could hear a lull in the music, and he could sense Don getting closer. One more curtain and he would be onto him like a foot on an ant.

It was time. Shit, stop thinking . . .

I always make women happy, ESP-ed Gary. He looked around. *Just ask anyone.*

He smiled at Bunnie. *Come here, let me show you.*

No, thought Bunnie. *Let me show you . . .*

"Can't wait," whispered Gary.

"Bet you can't," snapped Bunnie and, with a rugby-style push, toppled Gary into the band.

The music stopped . . .

The drum crashed to the ground.

The women stared . . .

Silence . . .

Legless jumped to attention and, with a "now or never" and a "ta-da," ripped the curtains open.

"It's me!" he shouted.

Silence . . .

"Sons, it's your old man," he said.

Nothing.

He stared at the sea of backs huddled about the front of the band.

"I thought it was a lull," he muttered.

Legless had expected gasps of shock, exclamations, but there wasn't even a *look*. He coughed for attention, and when none came, he looked across the room.

Beryl, circling a waltz with Ed, waved. She, still under the influence of strawberry *haze* tobacco, was so excited about dancing without going blind that the whole Gary episode went right over her head.

"Look at me," she said, laughing, "waltzing without glasses."

Legless needed a noise of epic proportion to make those in the room stand still.

He, preparing himself for his best Zaghareet call. He filled his lungs, cupped his hand over his mouth . . . and was just on the verge of letting forth when a woman grabbed his arm and, with a "make this sixty-year-old nurse live again," dragged him onto the floor.

Bollocks, thought Legless.

"Play something with a kick," she shouted. "A Jimmy Shand—I want to spin like that couple over there."

Nick, wrestling his drums upright, muttered a "hold your horses." Legless, thinking on his feet, shouted, "Agnes Waltz'!" and as the band fumbled into action, Legless slid his hand around the nurse's waist and guided her to the side of the room, preparing a dump at the hot chocolate table . . .

Forward one, two, three, four—back two, three, four—swirl around one, two, three, four . . .

She was having none of it; she took control and with a twirl maneuvered them away from the hot chocolate and into the center.

She didn't know who he was, but he was hers for this dance and, if she played her cards right, a lot more . . .

They waltzed until the song ended, capturing the attention of Beryl.

Let's try a foxtrot, thought Legless, *that'll clear the room . . .*

"Foxtrot? I'm looking for a bit more than that," snapped the nurse. "Give me a 'Bluebell Polka.'" She looked at her partner. "And you're going nowhere."

Chapter Twenty-Three

POT, PRUDENCE, AND POPE

"The planet was in the hands of a twenty-three-year-old with no idea about sex, bribery, or many other things that shifted power." —Verruca's memoirs

DBO looked from face to face. "You're not alone. We've got the big guns to help."

"Big guns—I thought that was us," muttered Pot.

"He means Pete," said Prudence.

"Him," huffed Pope. "Can't wait to see him."

"And, well, a man spy—*the* man spy," said DBO.

"Her," snapped an Alterationist.

"And of course Woody," said DBO.

"*The dwarf!*"

"*He's coming here?*"

"*To help us?*"

"Just need the Operators on our side," said DBO.

"And they don't know you're missing," said Prudence.

DBO attempted a "do I care" face.

"They still don't know you're missing?" said Vegas.

"Nope. Not one." She rolled up her instructions with a sniff. "I may as well have been a beverage cup in that shed, for all they cared."

Vegas, for the first time in her life, felt a pang of sympathy.

"All those years in the shed," she muttered.

"That could be to your advantage," muttered Pope.

A few women nodded sagely.

"Yes, invisibility helped us," said an Alterationist.

"And us," said Pope.

The wrinkled Alterationist patted Vegas's hand. "I like your diagrams."

"Thanks," muttered H2.

The wrinkled Alterationist stopped and looked at her comrades. "Why don't we make you a saving-the-planet outfit?"

The others nodded.

"There's no need for that." DBO blushed.

"You can't take over a planet looking like a worker. You need to look more, well, intellectual, dynamic. A haircut would help."

"We haven't time! We must make those Operators listen."

"Darl, by the time we've finished with you, even the scarecrows will listen."

As the Alterationist quickly rigged up an outfit for DBO in the ladies', Vegas and the 33 Robots decided the only thing to do was make a list.

Obvious to the "oops," "ouch," and "mind my hair" from the ladies, they wrote, crossed out, and argued until finally, DBO in a hemp hessian suit, or as Prudence called it, a "good old-fashioned potato sack," appeared.

Vegas looked up from her pad and started. "Not quite what we are looking for . . ." She turned to the robots. "Is it?"

Pope chuckled.

"Perhaps not one of our best," muttered an Alterationist.

DBO retreated as the robot's H-Pad rattled.

Verruca appeared on the screen.

Pot, mid doodling, jumped.

"Ma'am?"

"They have made contact with Earth—a tin opener and a dog," said Verruca.

"Tin opener?" Pot chuckled. "What on Earth is that?"

The other two robots fell about laughing.

"Earth—good one," muttered Prudence.

Vegas stared at the screen. "Who is that?"

"Verruca. She discovered the tin opener," muttered Pope.

"That's Verruca?" said Vegas.

"Don't let the wrinkles fool," whispered Prudence, "she has a mind that makes Hilda look comatose."

"She ran rings around the so-called establishment years ago," said the waitress, lifting the jug. "We would not be here if it weren't for her." She stopped. "Is that her? Haven't seen her in ages . . ." She peered into the screen. "You haven't changed a bit," she shouted.

Verruca nodded a thank-you as the waitress headed for the counter.

"She's aged," muttered the waitress to her comrade.

"Haven't we all," muttered the wrinkled Alterationist.

Verruca, ignoring the "aged" comment, told the robots to focus. She had kept in contact since they were outcast by the hippie colony to the veranda (which was pretty much the first day they arrived). Some said they were planted by her, a line she hotly denied.

"All they want is attention," so she said. The hippies did wonder—since when did a robot want attention?

DBO appeared, this time in an upmarket orange all-in-one suit with a belt for implements, LEADER written in capital letters across her left breast and back, her hair drawn back into a bun and glasses. She looked like an astronaut minus the helmet.

"We are ready to revolt," said Vegas with a salute.

Verruca almost smiled. The planet couldn't be in better hands.

"Well, you have your orders," she said.

"Orders?" muttered a few.

"Yes," said Verruca, and without waiting for a reply, she signed off with an "over and out."

The women looked about, confused.

DBO smiled. "Now all we need is H2 on the line."

"Stand at ease," repeated the automotive voice as a screen rose from the slit in the table.

"Who did that?" said the secretary.

They all looked at the H-Pad 11.

"Wasn't me," snapped the implement.

Woody, still on the default setting, appeared on the screen.

A few of the Operators brightened up until his handsome face phased out and Verruca's appeared.

"I know what you are thinking—"

"Doubt it," muttered the secretary.

"—that all you need to do is create another shed."

"There will never be another shed," muttered a voice from the back.

"Turn it down," said someone.

"Do you think that's a good idea?" muttered Deidre.

Operator Two slid the table drawer open, looking for some sort of volume control.

"Don't touch anything," said Verruca.

Operator Two eased the drawer shut.

"Your days of shed dwelling are over," said Verruca. "A new dawn has dawned, a new page has been turned, and you are part of this glorious new page—an integral cog in the wheels of Planet Hy Man's history."

Silence . . .

"Any minute now, H2 and DBO will be contacting you."

Operator One stopped. *That's who's missing!*

DBO and Vegas looked up from their H-Pad and turned to the women in the canteen.

"Are you with us?"

"Yes!"

"Shall we move forward?"

"Yes!"

"Finally a utopia is in the making," said DBO.

Chapter Twenty-Four

WOODY

"A good man always knows how to keep a secret." –Archie

Mex, H2, Pete, and Woody stood in the corner of the courtyard of greatness, inches from the statue of Manifesto the Great. It was nighttime; there was no one about, apart from those in the marketplace outside the courtyard gates. They were packing up and liked to make a meal of it. Being of lower class, there wasn't much else to look forward to but packing up, so it was a time of joshing, shouting, and tossing leftovers at each other.

"Cop this!"

"Cop that!"

"Cop it yourself—I'd rather have my ears pricked!"

Mex fumbled for her key card. Her man spy pad was not far. She looked at Pete.

"You had them last, ma'am," he said.

The women in the café were all revved up for a revolution, or "coup," as the waitress called it. They waited with anticipation, staring at the designated landing pad just shy of the delicatessen table.

It was Prudence's idea. "Always good to have a snack handy after telespraying," she said.

No one questioned her, they were all too excited. Meeting a man from Earth is not something a woman from the hippie colony dreamt of, let alone a dwarf, and here they were, *waiting . . .*

Their hot chocolates were going cold and they didn't even care!

Any minute, Woody would be telesprayed and tucking into a soya cheese spread. *Who cared about hot drinks?*

"Do humans tuck in?" muttered an Alterationist.

"We'll soon find out," muttered the waitress.

They waited . . .

And waited . . .

And waited, and when nothing happened apart from DBO swearing into her H-Pad, they grumbled.

"Pickling coordinates," muttered DBO, "forgot about Pete and his Teflon."

"Teflon," muttered Pope. "It's a given."

DBO, Vegas, and Prudence turned to Pope. "A given?" they said in unison.

"Always buggers telespraying up," muttered Pope.

"Now you tell us," snapped Vegas.

"Yes sirree, you can't trust that Teflon when it comes to telespraying."

"So why didn't you say?" said DBO.

"You never asked."

"We are trying to save the planet and you are waiting to be asked?" said Vegas.

"You have never needed to be asked before," muttered Pot.

Pope looked about the accusing faces. "We are designed for asking," he said. "Not thinking."

The waitress tutted. "Thinking, that's all you ever do. That's why we keep you outside. Too smart for your own good."

"Nothing queerer than robots," muttered an Alterationist.

"Shhhh," said Vegas. Mex and Pete could be heard arguing on the H-Pad.

Woody's profile flashed up on DBO's H-Pad screen. Behind it was Hilda's half-finished statue.

The women crowded around.

"Look at his hair," muttered one.

"Look at that statue," said an Alterationist.

"Must be one of those Rastafarians," said the waitress.

"Oooh, love to meet one of them," said Prudence.

"Reefers the size of carrots," said Pot with a laugh.

"Size? Look at the size of that nose," said an Alterationist.

"You could ski on it," said the voice from the back.

As Pete and Mex argued, H2 flicked through her H-Pad for connections. Woody, unused to telespraying, had materialized with a sharp intake of breath and a bounce. He stopped, patted down his body with an "I'm still all in one piece" look, and then stared.

Was he actually on another planet? Still alive?

He jumped, skipped, and twisted . . .

Still working.

He sniffed, scratched, and coughed . . .

All okay.

He stopped, looked about, kicked at the gravel . . .

It was a bit like Earth.

Then he caught sight of Manifesto the Great's statue, loosely covered in a scratchy hemp cloth. It flapped in the breeze. He peered underneath, marveling at the size of its appendages.

A man? thought Woody with sniff. *And a funny odor, like play dough.* Then he spied a plaque embedded into the statues' giant feet.

The Great Manifesto

The inventor of the Manifesto, the manual and the dictionary.

He took writing to another level.

He broke the mold and reset it again.

The one, the only . . .

The rest was scratched out.

Woody sniffed. *Play dough and something else—grass?* He reached to touch the feet.

"No touching of statues," said a robotic voice.

Woody jumped.

"Recycled material . . . takes centuries to harden."

Woody felt a rumble in his pocket.

He pulled out his Nokia. It pulsated green, red, and fluorescent yellow.

"Recycled, but not as you know it," said the Nokia.

Woody looked at his phone; it had been transformed into a sleek, hand-size device with only one button.

"I am completely voice controlled," said the Nokia, "and I must say it feels very nice."

Woody stopped listening to the distant rabble of the marketplace.

"Cop this, luv!"

"Luv? I ain't nobody's luv!"

"Ha-ha, Nobody's Luv—you're a hoot!"

The Nokia, now in full reading-minds-and-being-informative mode, began to explain about the market, its barter system, and the whole "if you don't get half the asking price you have been robbed" philosophy.

"Is this the future for Earth?" said Woody.

"It is but a given," said the Nokia.

"I see," muttered Woody, his senses tingling. The atmosphere, as the Nokia put it, took a while to adjust to.

"Perhaps a walk, dear Woody, a meander to get your sea legs, so to speak."

Woody meandered about the great statues and stopped at Hilda's statue.

He thought about his home and his family. All his life, he had been waiting for something to happen, something better than a video on Saturday night in his flat and roast chicken on Sunday with his family.

In fact, the last time he saw his family was at a Sunday roast. He was still reeling from seeing Mex at the bus shelter, trying to convince himself it was a mirage, a dream, a hallucination. He knew it wasn't, and as he sat around his mother's table, he could not erase the thoughts from his mind. Finally compelled to search, he stood up from the table without touching his greens.

"I'm heading out, Ma, got things to do."

His brothers sniggered.

"I may not be back for some time."

"Aye right," said his brothers in unison.

"And if I'm not—"

"I'll keep your dinner in the oven for you," said his mother.

Woody's tummy rumbled. He wondered if his food was still in the oven.

His mother's cooking had a lot to answer for. Being healthy was one thing, but not being able to move without a fanfare from your innards was taking it too far. But would she listen?

"Mother texted," said Nokia.

"What?" said Woody.

"Mother contacted, reassured. She thinks you're somewhere learning to write."

"I see. Maybe I could send her a photo," he muttered. "Or would that—"

"Done," said the Nokia.

"—scare her?" Woody looked at the Nokia's screen. "Shit, you sent her a picture?"

"Of the statue—the face, actually, the profile."

"That nose? It's like a mountain range. Why did you send her that? I was thinking of a selfie, something more Earth-like . . ."

The Nokia beeped: a text.

You could ski off that, texted Woody's mother.

"Ski?" said Woody.

"Skiing is not permissible," said a voice from the dark shadows.

Woody looked about. H2, Mex, and Pete were engaged in conversation on their H-Pad; the only other person was a footman dozing in the corner.

Was it him? thought Woody.

The footman let out a robust snore.

❇

"Looks like a change of plan," muttered Vegas.

"If a dwarf won't go to the café, then the café must come to the dwarf," said DBO.

"Of course," said the waitress. "We can only do all this if those robots over there are out of the way."

"Me?" said Pope and Pot in unison.

"I understand him and him," said Prudence, pointing. "But me? What have I done?"

DBO turned to them. "We could do with you in the city. There is, after all, paperwork."

"Paperwork? Me?" muttered Pope.

"And you get to meet Pete again, won't that be fun?"

"Pfff," muttered Pope.

Chapter Twenty-Five

HILDA'S SIESTA

"The only thing important about a name is who remembers it." – DBO

It was Vegas's idea to contact the Operators, and it was the Operators' idea to send Alice to the courtyard of greatness.

None of them wanted to face H2 or DBO. After finally working out who the missing two were, they, shamefaced, recalled how the others had treated the two of them . . . cutting them out of beverage breaks, closing the shed while they were still in it, and, even worse, not remembering their names.

In fact, if it weren't for Alice, they still wouldn't have known.

"You should be ashamed of yourselves," said the H-Pad 11.

"It's not something we're proud of," muttered Operator Four.

"I mean how were we to know?" said Operator Two.

"What?" said the H-Pad 11. "That two tea-making Operators whose names you don't even know could explore the Black Hills, Earth *and* not only make it back but sound like they knew what they were doing."

Silence . . .

"They're talking of a coup," said the H-Pad 11.

"I thought only men did coups," muttered the Operator Four.

"Obviously not," said Operator One with a glance at her troops. She looked at Alice circling the room, tidying up cups and papers. "What we need is a diversionary plan."

"Prolong, divert, and irritate," muttered the secretary. "Something that will annoy DBO and H2 so much that by the time they meet up with us"—she looked at Alice—"they'll be relieved rather than—"

"Pissed off," muttered a voice from the back.

Alice stopped. "Are you implying that I annoy?"

Silence . . .

"I find that rather offensive."

"It's a long shot," said the H-Pad 11. "But it's pretty much the only shot you have."

It was Woody Alice approached first. She flew into the courtyard of greatness, spied H2, Mex, and Pete talking to DBO on the H-Pad, and then saw Woody.

She was still smarting from the annoying comments and desperate to prove them wrong. She figured a man from Earth standing on his own would appreciate a little help.

Before Woody had time to reply to his mother's text or stop his Nokia from sending another picture, Alice, suspended in air, was tapping on Woody's shoulder.

He turned to see a robotic appendage retract into a golden metallic ball the size of a watermelon, with two beams shining out from two slots and what looked like a smile underneath.

Alice, suspended in the air, was inches from his face.

"I am Alice," she said.

"Alice?"

"A robot, but not as you'd know it," said Nokia.

Alice stopped. "What was that?"

"A mobile, but not as you'd know it," said the Nokia.

"Oh," said Alice. She jigged up and down. "You have one of those? I have heard of these mobile phones." She zoomed in on the Nokia in Woody's hand.

For a moment, there seemed to Woody to be a connection that didn't include him.

"What are you doing?" he said.

"Nothing . . ." said the Nokia and Alice in unison.

"Funny kind of nothing," muttered Woody.

"It's time to move on," said Alice.

"To the next level?" said Nokia.

"Yes," whispered Alice.

Woody was about to ask *Where, why, and just now?* when Alice let out a wolf whistle, jolting awake the dozing footman.

Pete looked up, followed by Mex and H2.

"Alice," muttered H2.

"Alice," sighed Mex.

Pete groaned.

H2 looked at her H-Pad. "The Operators have sent Alice."

"Alice?" said DBO. "I thought she was out of action, suspended under the Interference Act."

"Hilda doesn't believe in that Act," said Vegas.

"How are we to save the planet with her poking her nose in?" said Mex.

Alice shot across the yard and stopped inches from Mex's nose. "I am here to help, not hinder."

"Help? You tell everyone everything. You have as much chance of keeping a secret as Pete here has of becoming a woman."

Pete, clutching his bag of Primark clothes, stopped. "Who said anything about becoming a woman?"

"It's nothing to be ashamed of," said H2. She turned to the H-Pad. "The Operators have probably sent her as a diversionary tactic. As if I am that easily diverted."

"The Operators are under my command," butted in Alice.

They looked at her with an I-find-that-hard-to-believe look . . .

"Well, they are . . . they just don't know it yet. You ask Hilda."

"Hilda is on holiday," said DBO.

"Not exactly a holiday," said Alice.

It was then that Verruca intervened.

Hilda had no idea what was going on, and even if she did, she was enjoying herself too much to care. She was experiencing pleasure for the first time, and she was hooked, addicted like a crack addict. Verruca had designed the ultimate vibrator, the sort that had more twist and turns than a soap opera, and it endlessly surprised Hilda—surprises that were way better than any package opening. In fact, she could think of nothing else but the next surprise.

Hilda, for the first time, was experiencing a happiness that did not involve the destruction of another woman's plans, and she didn't want it to stop.

Verruca sat in her kitchen. She had just been through her drawers and discovered batteries that should have been in Hilda's vibrator; instead they were in her hand, and the robot was explaining why.

Basically, he had forgotten them.

"This cuts the time," said Verruca. "These were self-charging; the more you used them, the more they charged. What has she got?"

"The recycled ones."

"Great pickling *pomegranate*."

"How much time for the switchover?" said Verruca.

The robot counted on his fingers.

Verruca lost patience. "All right, we must swap batteries. It's our only chance."

She did a time check to see who was where and quickly adjusted her plans. "I'm heading into the city," she said.

"Shall I pack, ma'am?" said the robot.

"No, not necessary."

The robot moved to follow her.

"And you can stay here."

"Ma'am?"

Verruca, with an impatient gesture towards the fridge, said, "And clean the fridge."

Hilda, sprawled out on her bed like a Middle Eastern dancer with a bad hairdo, sighed. Her pelvis was literally singing. A few days ago it was a stranger, a part of her body she covered up after a quick wash-down, a place unthought of let alone talked of.

Now she couldn't take her hands off it and all the glorious, juicy bits and pieces that pulsated beneath.

She wondered about a name. *Cupcake?*

She smiled. *Delicious.*

Chocolate, cherry, cream puff?

She giggled, rolled over, and looked at her so-called drill. *Perhaps that could do with a new name too.*

Percy? Percival? Mr Pecker?

The battery light flashed . . .

What?

She pressed it . . .

Nothing.

She shook it . . .

Still nothing.

"Alice!" she shouted.

There was no reply, only her voice echoing through the empty corridor.

Chapter Twenty-Six

THE CHANGE

"The stuff of Legends is nothing more than the stuff of Myths." – The H-Pad 11

H2, in her Operator jumpsuit, strode through the dusty path of the market with Alice in her backpack. Behind her marched Mex, Pete, and, at the rear, Woody.

Everyone stopped mid packing up and stared; the laughter, the bartering, the joshing silenced as the end of the day food sizzled, forgotten . . .

Never before had an Operator been seen to march down the market lane, let alone with a man spy—man spies walked alone, possibly with a robot behind them, but never with an Operator.

They watched, then gasped when Woody came into view, who, to quote one, "walked like a god."

"*A dwarf?*"

"*So handsome!*"

"*So young!*"

Dwarves were the stuff of legends, especially one so young. The only men the women saw were the old, wrinkled footmen dozing by the gates of the courtyard of greatness. They had no idea that a man with no wrinkles existed, let alone one so deliciously short.

H2 and her entourage passed the stalls of tofu, hemp, and beads as the women sighed over Woody.

His senses pumped with adrenaline.

He was in God knows where, hit by smells of God knows what, amongst hungry-looking peasant women who looked so tough they could bite the head off a rattlesnake.

Pete told Woody he was forbidden fruit, as "illegal as creamy coffee," intimidating Woody so much he couldn't even think of a swear word.

They passed the market band packing up, the only three women not to notice Woody.

The market band played old kitchenware—pots and pans—for money. Today they had made enough to buy beverages for two . . . and in the midst of deciding who was to go without, they didn't see H2's entourage. They continued to clatter and pack until a deaf old woman bending over a campfire looked up and shouted, "A dwarf?"

Pans crashed to the ground as the elderly woman stopped Woody with her stick.

H2, Mex, and Pete, unaware, carried on.

Woody stared at the blackened tofu oozing over the end of the stick bubbling with smoke—it looked anything but appetizing.

The old woman smiled, crinkling her black face.

"A person of short statue," she said.

He nodded with a nervous smile. She nodded back.

Woody made to keep moving with a decisive stride and was stopped by a stall holder.

She gestured with a set of beads. "For you," she said.

Woody shook his head with a smile and made for a more militant march but was stopped by another stall holder, and before he had a chance to administer a firm but polite brush-off, another jumped in front, thrusting a hemp scarf in his face.

Then another offering *soap?*

"*Burger?*" said another.

"*Hemp cream?*" said another.

Within seconds, Woody's path was blocked by women the height of basketball players and Pete was nowhere to be seen. He peered through their legs.

Where the bollocking hell were they?

He caught sight of Pete's back disappearing behind a corner.

"Pete!" he shouted just as the market band started up.

"You want to hear a song?" they shouted.

Woody, surrounded by a women, could not see a thing.

"Peeeete!" he yelled.

Alice lit up, jumping to attention. *Woody?*

"Pete, come back!!!"

Alice revved into autopilot, overriding H2's shutdown program. She burst from the backpack—*her hero needed her.*

Mex stopped and turned.

The woman gasped . . .

H2 looked at Mex.

Mex, instantly in man spy mode, moved to run.

H2 stopped her.

Mex looked at her with a "you're stopping *me?*" glare.

The onlookers watched and waited. *Perhaps a fight?*

Alice cut through the crowd like a gigantic unwanted fly. Woman dodged as she flew in and out of the stalls, annoying all. Some tutted, others tried to swat her.

"Nokia, I am coming," she shouted as the old woman with the tofu on a stick took a swipe.

Alice dodged.

A band member lifted her broom/beater, another a pan lid; Alice swerved one, dodged the other—straight into the old lady's upheld stick, who, like an expert batsman, sent Alice flying into the side of the canvas wall of a stall.

Tofu splattered onto Alice like a custard-pie fight.

Alice, gagging, ricocheted off the canvas and crashed into a heap of beads.

Woody, with great care, rescued her. "There was no need for that," he said, picking off bits of tofu.

Alice blinked at Woody. "Is the Nokia okay?"

Woody, now surrounded by women apologizing, was about to say "yes" and more when his Nokia sprung from his pocket.

"I am here!" The Nokia said, sending Alice into jigs of joy.

Woody stared out into a sea of women. All focus was on him and what he was going to do next . . .

Alice, like *her* hero the Nokia, thought on her feet. She turned to the band . . .

"Soon you'll have real instruments to play," she said, gesturing towards the scatter of pans with great ceremony, "instead of these cooking pots."

The band gasped, the women stopped in their tracks . . .

Real instruments?

There had been talk of such things, but no one had ever seen one, except perhaps the old lady by the fire.

"Aye, real instruments," said the old lady. "A sight to behold, almost as much as a dwarf."

And, with a loud cackle, she blew out her fire.

The Operators, waiting for the arrival of H2 and DBO, organized a spread, along with sparkling water and hot beverages. The Operators were in a tizzy; not only were they trying to make decisions and look like they knew what they were doing, but now with H2 and DBO in the mix, they, to quote BBC Sport, had been "thrown a curve ball," a "googly."

DBO and H2 seemed to know more about saving the planet than the rest of the Operators put together. In fact, the Operators hadn't even realized the planet needed saving until word of Hilda and her drill got out.

The Operators thought they had been caught in a reshuffle of power, and despite the ordering of supplies for the kitchen and the mastering of bartering, they still hoped the general order of things would, in due course, resume.

"All I ever wanted was a decent beverage," said Operator Four. "Not all this organizing, taking-care-of-things malarkey."

"And now we're supposed to be saving the planet?" muttered Operator Two.

"I think that is H2 and DBO's job," muttered the secretary.

Operator One spied a footman smirking at the door and was just about to make a "wipe that smile off your face" comment when Alice could be seen whizzing up the marketplace on their H-Pad 11.

"They'll be looking for an apology," muttered Operator Four.

"And how is that done without looking like a pickling tit in front of that damnable Deidre?" hissed Operator Two.

The Operators eyed the reporter, who, pad poised, was asking the footman about the whereabouts of Hilda's personal footman, who requiring the odd prodding to keep awake.

"What if we get rid of her?" whispered the secretary.

"Bit drastic," said Operator One.

"Drastic—that woman will be taking down notes and spreading the word about us. We'll be the joke of the century. Imagine how it will look: Operator One on her knees waiting for a "yes I forgive" by H2 and DBO, or worse, a written report."

Operator One looked about. "Why me? Why should I be on my knees?"

The others, ignoring her, continued.

"I don't see what a report has to do with things," said Operator Four.

"You never know," muttered another.

"Yes, but getting rid? Is that how we roll?" muttered another.

"Roll? What are you talking about?"

"You know . . . is that how we do things now? Get rid of the likes of . . ." She nodded towards Deidre.

"I am talking of finding her somewhere to investigate, a ruse," said the secretary.

The other Operators breathed a sigh of relief.

"That's easy, ma'am," muttered a footman, lifting a few empty plates. "Hilda is shouting for Alice," he said.

The Operators looked at him. Where had they seen him before?

Deidre looked up. "What are you up to?"

"We are just discussing Hilda and her holiday," said Operator One.

Chapter Twenty-Seven

WATCHING

"There's colonies, there's the outpost, and then there's something in between called a field." —A stall worker

H2 and Mex watched as Woody appeared, along with a dark-faced old lady brandishing a stick of equally dark tofu and a mile-long fan club behind her.

"What will we do with all them?" muttered Mex.

"Educate," said H2.

"Educate?" said Mex and Pete together.

Mex stared at the elderly woman at the front. She wore the flowing robes of Dumbledore and the blacked-out face of a minstrel performer, while brandishing her stick like it was a weapon.

"That'll lead to nothing but trouble," muttered Mex.

H2 jumped up onto a set of boxes. Her foot broke through, followed by the rest of her; as she disappeared into the boxes, the fan club laughed.

Woody quieted the fan club with a "give her some space" gesture as Pete and Mex helped her out.

"Perhaps you should head off," said Mex, "do the speech later? That lot has the concentration of a stick insect."

H2, ignoring Mex, jumped onto a stall and looked at the sun-bleached faces.

"We have been to Earth and back," she shouted.

"Earth?"

"What the pickle is Earth?"

"Earth is where he comes from," said the old woman, pointing burnt tofu at Woody.

"I thought it was a myth, a story," said a voice from the back.

"So did we all," said another.

Mex pulled out her pocket-size whip, causing great laughter from the women.

"Oooh, big whip for a man spy."

"Come and tickle us."

"What's wrong with small?" shouted Woody.

Silence . . .

"Does anyone have a problem with things that are . . . small?"

A few muttered . . .

"Speak up."

Silence.

"Shall we continue?"

Most nodded, and Woody, with great ceremony, gestured for H2 to continue.

H2 looked out onto the expectant faces and talked of what she saw on Earth, of a world where workers sold things to the likes of Beryl "face to face," and how the likes of Beryl walked amongst the likes of "us."

"We could have that here: a new world, a world where the market would be given the place it deserves," along with decent hemp cashmere rather than "that cheap soya jersey you lot are forced to wear."

"Steady on, I made this," said a woman at the front.

"Very nice," muttered Woody.

The woman at the front beamed.

"I am talking of a coup," said H2.

"What's that?" yelled a voice from the back.

"A car from so-called Earth," laughed another.

"An uprising," said the old lady with a flip of her cape.

A few tutted, some muttered . . .

"Go back to your shed," yelled a voice from the back.

H2 stopped. *Confusion is what ruined the planet. She must enlighten, educate, and inspire.*

"There is no shed," she shouted.

Silence . . .

"No shed?" shouted one.

"And the leader's on holiday," shouted Mex.

"Holiday?" shouted the same one. "That's not what I heard. I thought she was incognito like all those others at the top—don't you listen to Deidre?"

"Yes, and just when did Deidre get it right? Remember her talks of Legless, stuff of legends?" said the old lady.

The women looked at each other . . .

"*Who?*"

"*Legless?*"

"*Who's he when he's at home?*"

"*Something to do with a bike?*"

"*Pfff, that old pickled walnut.*"

H2, unfazed, continued. She had faced worse.

All her stinking life she had been invisible, talked over, laughed at —well, not anymore. She was going to make a difference, save every single invisible woman just like her—starting with the market women —*and they could like it or lump it.*

H2 talked of comrades, workers' rights, equality, and how things could be better, which in the market vendors' line of work didn't take much. It was a speech she'd practiced many times in her head, along with a picture of a jubilant "viva la workers" reaction, and as she stared into the faces of the women below, she realized she needed to do more.

H2 inhaled . . . "A new world, a new order, and the Building of Opulence will be like an open book."

"*Book?*"

"*What's she on about?*"

"We just need to make a few tweaks," H2 added.

Tweaks?

"Adjustments," shouted Mex.

"Revolution!" shouted H2 with an air punch.

"Revolution?" said a musician. "Give me a set of drums and I'll be happy."

"And Woody," laughed a voice from the back.

"Not everyone wants revolution," muttered the old lady.

"Guess not," muttered H2.

"Perhaps Ma'am could make things a tad simpler," said Pete.

"Don't call me ma'am," Said H2.

"He has a point," said Alice.

"Perhaps a slogan, something to chant?" said Pete.

"What you need is a short, sharp shock," muttered the old lady. "Urgency . . . without putting the fear of God into—"

"The planet is going to implode into darkness," shouted Woody.

The women gasped.

"Implode—is that the same as explode?"

"We're exploding?"

"Exploding when?"

They started to panic . . .

"My mice."

"My washing."

"I'm too young to die."

"So much more hemp to—"

"Great pickling tofu, why were we never warned?" shouted a voice from the back.

Woody jumped up onto the stall, cleared the decks with a swift kick, held up his hands with a "shut it and listen to me" gesture, and shouted, "If . . ."

He looked for silence.

"If . . ." He shouted louder: "IF!!!!"

Silence.

"We don't act now, take this chance . . ." Woody looked at the blank faces. They didn't have a clue. "Your energy supply is running dry," he shouted.

The women sighed with relief . . .

"That old chestnut."

"They are always saying that."

"Tell us something new."

"Big flaming pickle."

"Why didn't you say so in the first place instead of all this comrades end-of-the-world bollocks? We've been saying that for years: energy from a spark plug." The musician huffed. "Only a moron would rely on a spark plug."

"There's colonies out there you know," said a voice from the back.

"Hippies and things," said a musician.

"Fish and scarecrows," shouted another voice from the back.

"And can we explore, connect? Can we pickle?"

"We're forbidden to connect, locked in the city, trapped like soya beans in a tin, while those who rule are up there living it up."

"Yeah!"

"Too right!"

"Connecting with them would be a piece of hemp," said the drummer.

"Ma'am," interrupted Alice.

"Not now."

"Ma'am?"

"Call me H2." She stopped; Alice was jigging up and down like a tot desperate for the toilet. H2's face softened. "Can't it wait?" she whispered.

"Deidre is leaving the room with a view."

"Great pickling pomegranate," said the old lady.

Chapter Twenty-Eight

ALICE

"The best-laid plans of Mice and H-Pads often go unnoticed." —H-Pad Template

H2 and Mex stood in front of the Building of Opulence. Their plan was to take over the room with a view and connect DBO to it, while the market women manually connected with the hippies and their energy. It was a simple enough plan that had most impressed—apart from the old lady, who seemed to have disappeared.

Under the insistence of the market women, Woody, along with his Nokia and a spare set of plans, stayed behind. Pete, fearing for his soul mate's virtue, stayed with him.

H2 and Mex made their way to the Building of Opulence, and if it wasn't for the impending doom weighing on H2's and Mex's shoulders, they probably would have noticed the old lady reappear from behind a stall and follow with out-of-date incognito tactics.

The entrance was a grand facade of glass and revolving doors. Footmen stood at the front as young, official-looking women left the building and cleaner robots entered: the changing of the shift was taking place.

Leading up to the entrance was an impressive flight of stairs, which the young women silently raced down and the cleaning robots trudged up, some on rollers, making the-getting-up-the-stairs process painful to watch.

"We need to catch these woman before they finish," said H2.

"Catch?" said Mex. "Wouldn't it be better to wait until they're gone? Convincing that lot won't be as easy as those market morons."

H2 inhaled . . . "A new world, a new order. The Building of Opulence will be an open book. "

"So you keep saying," muttered Mex.

"And the word *moron* banished."

"They will still be morons," muttered Mex.

"We need to explain," said H2.

"Explain? What, that they will be less important now? That we are taking over? That all their sucking up, groveling, and unpaid overtime has gotten them nowhere?"

"She has a point, ma'am," said Alice.

"Perhaps Ma'am should take things a tad slower," said Mex with her newly acquired Earth irony.

H2, with a "don't call me ma'am" on the tip of her tongue, caught sight of the old lady sliding behind a footman at the bottom of the stairs. Mex followed her eyes. "Where did she spring from?"

"No idea."

"Such rubbish spy techniques," muttered Mex.

H2 laughed. "Probably from the BBC, those police stories. Us Operators couldn't get enough of 'em for a while."

She stopped; nostalgic memories flooded back.

"Come on," said Mex, "we can easily lose her when we go in."

They raced like army cadets up the side of the stairs and hid behind a pillar, waiting for a robot. A squat turtle-shaped robot on rollers rolled by. H2 motioned to Mex to hide behind the turtle-shaped robot. Mex motioned back. "You're shorter," she hissed.

"So?"

Mex pulled out her whip. "I've got this."

H2, with a thanks-for-nothing face, squatted behind the robot, inching forward at a snail's pace.

Mex, now full of her man-spy senses, unleashed her miniature whip into the air. It wrapped around a pillar. She, like Spiderman, sailed through a window, dropping behind a footman, her breasts pressed against his back.

"Oh," he said, startled.

She moved to the side; he nodded. "Man spy practice again, ma'am?"

"Exactly." She laughed, saluting at the two women left in the foyer.

H2, still outside the doors, squinted from behind her miniature robot, pulling back with a "shit" as a couple of young sleek women trotted by.

The robot inched forward. H2, getting impatient, turned to see an upright robot heading up the stairs.

She waited . . .

It stopped.

She made to move behind the upright robot, but the old lady got in first.

H2, with a mouthful of *pickling* swear words, crouched behind the turtle-shaped robot.

Another young woman trotted by.

Bollocking pickle!

The old lady and the robot trotted past.

Bollocking pickled walnut!

H2 inched a look over the robot's shoulder and looked into the foyer.

The foyer was empty apart from Mex dusting off a footman in a jocular manner, a young woman briskly packing up her H-Pad, and another tossing a disposable cup into a recycling bin with precise aim. They were young, sleek, and solemn, and neither noticed as the old lady slipped through the revolving doors behind the upright robot.

"Ma'am," said Alice.

"I said don't call me—"

"She's slid in."

"Who?" said H2.

"The old lady."

"Great shitting walnut," said H2.

The old lady slid from the robot to the water cooler.

I've seen that slide of a walk before, thought H2. *So familiar . . .*

Her H-Pad flashed. "Vegas said you need to use the back entrance," said DBO.

"Affirmative," whispered H2.

Mex caught sight of H2 at the entrance on her knees like a floor scrubber. *You see the old lady,* she mouthed to H2, *behind the beverage cooler?*

H2 nodded. It was then that H2 noticed something odd: the old lady's black face was dripping . . .

The old lady caught sight of H2; their eyes locked. *I know you,* thought H2.

The two young women headed for the exit. Mex could tell by the name tag that they were cadet Voted Ins.

"Can't believe she's still on holiday," said one.

"Me neither . . . do you think she's got a tan?" said the other.

"Pfff, Hilda? Very droll."

As they headed out of the revolving door, the old lady gestured for H2 to come. H2 began to crawl. Then, realizing no one was there, she stood up.

"Get down," hissed the old lady.

H2 collapsed like there was a shooting. Then, wondering why, she stood up.

"Cameras," hissed the old lady.

"Over there," gestured Mex.

H2 moved to what she thought was out of the camera's range.

"And there," snapped Mex.

The old lady grabbed H2 by the jacket and pulled her to the water cooler. H2 stared into a face covered in sticky black hemp effluent.

"Who are you?" said H2. She sniffed her face. "Is that what I think it is?"

"Could be," muttered the old lady.

H2 pulled a face and was about to launch into her "stay here and let us save the planet" speech when the old lady pulled the hood from her head and wiped her face with the trail of her clock.

"Verruca?"

"Batteries," said Verruca. "We need to get them to Hilda before Deidre does. God knows what hemp effluent she's going to tell her."

❄

Hilda, like a crack addict looking for a fix, stuck her head out of her penthouse door. The footman took one look at her matted "I've been rolling around my bed for a month" hair and looked away.

"Alice!" shouted Hilda. "Where the sperm are you?"

Alice, in shutdown mode in H2's backpack, lit up, activated by Hilda's voice.

"It's time," said Verruca.

"Must I," sighed Alice.

Verruca handed her four batteries.

Chapter Twenty-Nine

BLACK AND WHITE

"Blacking out and coloring in can be easily confused." – Explaining English Volume 1

*H*ilda retreated from the passageway and looked about. *Did she have any batteries?*

Then she saw her "something unusual" spy channel flashing.

"Old lady, black-and-white minstrel face, peering from water cooler."

What the son of sperm? "Show me a picture," snapped Hilda.

"Picture prevented—spy lock-down."

"Black-and-white minstrel," muttered Hilda. It sounded familiar. *Who would black their face to peer? No spy . . .*

Then it hit her. *Verruca? Pickling Verruca—she just couldn't help herself, could she?*

H2 crouched incognito style and looked about. *Did she hear something, a "son of" what?*

She looked at Mex; Mex shrugged.

"Spy lock-down," muttered Verruca.

The two women looked at her. *Lock-down?*

"The shed?" hissed Verruca. "The explosion?"

"Explosion?" Mex and H2 looked at each other. "The shed?"

"Can't have been pretty," muttered Mex.

Verruca gestured to the large *Hilda-shaped* clock face in the foyer. "We haven't much time." She motioned the two to move. "Hilda's up to her shenanigans again."

"Shenanigans?" mouthed Mex to H2.

"Get me Alice," Hilda shouted at her screen, then stopped. "No, wait a minute, can you record?"

"Ma'am, recording requires monitoring. It is but the same thing as viewing."

"Then coordinates—can you find any for the H-Pad 11?"

"Coordinates assembled, ma'am."

"Can you connect?"

"Connecting with that thing is but a piece of pie."

The H-Pad 11 jumped. "Ma'am, you have resurrected, so to speak."

"Yes," said Hilda, "and I want you to follow Verruca."

"Ma'am?"

"She's heading your way, you need to intercept."

"Interception commencing."

"Unnoticed."

"Oh."

"And while you're at it, find me some batteries."

Hilda rubbed her head; she was starting to feel her old self again. What was she thinking, all that rolling around on the bed hiding from the world?

All she needed was a mask to hide her face. No one would notice; she could still rule.

She pulled out her Darth Vader outfit and was about to slip on her mask when she caught sight of the drill package in the bin. She'd never noticed the note before.

She pulled it out and stopped . . .

"To the best leader ever!"

Oh, ha-ha, Verruca, very funny . . .

While the others were coercing Deidre out the door with talks of the next best story, the secretary watched the H-Pad 11 jolt like she'd swallowed a wasp. A rare movement for any H-Pad, let alone an "upcycled" H-Pad 11.

The secretary's mind pictured the H-Pad 11 template. *There was only one reason any H-Pad jolted like that, and it had nothing to do with wasps.*

She watched as the H-Pad 11 slid under the table, behind a chair, inches from the ground like a weasel. *It was heading for the door.*

Deidre, convinced that the Operators were talking bollocks and also convinced she had no choice, made to leave. The H-Pad 11 posed at the exit, waiting like a hovering terrier at a rabbit hole . . .

The door opened.

The H-Pad 11 shifted.

The door shut.

Deidre turned. "You sure a piece about Hilda's up-and-coming hairdo is really what people want to hear?"

The Operators nodded.

The door opened.

The H-Pad 11 scurried.

Deidre, not seeing the H-Pad 11, kicked it.

The H-Pad 11 hit the wall.

The door shut.

"Are you sure Hilda asked for me?"

"Yes, now go."

Deidre opened the door. The H-Pad 11 made a dash; still dazed, it hit a wall. The secretary, with a "just a cotton-picking minute," made a grab . . .

The H-Pad 11 shot from her hands down the corridor.

The footmen outside jolted awake, one being H2's shed-sharing footman. He slung his lace hankie over the H-Pad 11 as it flew by. The H-Pad 11 spluttered, coughed, and crashed to the ground.

The secretary followed, grabbed the H-Pad 11, tossed the hankie to the side, then stopped, picked it up, and, clutching the H-Pad 11 with all her strength, wrapped it in the hankie.

The H-Pad 11 jolted, and when that didn't work, it oozed hemp oil from the tip of its pencil. It dribbled onto the secretary's hands; the secretary fumbled and swore, then shouted for help as the hankie fell to the side.

The others looked up, then raced to the door as the H-Pad 11 shot its pencil into the secretary's arm. Before the secretary could shout "ow," another flew at her.

More pencils followed.

The secretary clung like an octopus on a leg. There was no way she was letting this upcycled upstart escape.

She yelled again as the Operators, dodging a stream of pencils, approached like gladiators into a ring.

The H-Pad 11 panicked; the last thing it wanted was to be back in the basement, shut down like all the rest. It had one last trick up its applicator.

Mice . . .

Within seconds, the floor was flooded with mechanical mice of all shapes and noises. The Operators dodged, tripped, and swore; the footmen uselessly flicked and tossed lace hankies while the H-Pad 11, feeling smug, slid from the secretary's hands and flew down the corridor.

The secretary made a useless grab, skidded on a pencil, and toppled to the floor as the H-Pad 11, now out of arm's reach, continued a stream of writing implements like a machine gun until even the footmen began to retreat.

"Fall back," shouted Operator Three, filling a cup with water. "I have seen these things before," she shouted, flinging water at the mice. "I'll toss, you run."

H2's footman, mid dodge of a crayon, grabbed the secretary and followed the others skidding and sidestepping back to the room with a view—a few collecting pencils on the way.

While Mex and H2 made their way to the room with a view, Verruca made her way to Hilda's room. She raced through the staff john, out a window, and up a fire escape, stopping to catch her breath when she realized she was lost.

"In here," shouted Alice, pulling the elderly woman through a shaft.

Verruca dusted herself down.

"I take it you haven't been in this building for a while?" said Alice.

Verruca, still breathless, nodded. "Back in the days when men were anything but a footman."

Alice took her to Hilda's floor.

As they arrived at one end of the corridor, the H-Pad 11 arrived at the other. The corridor was long, with corners and alcoves for sitting, plotting, and sipping chilled water. Verruca stared down the glossy corridor wide enough for a car and light enough to get a suntan. The ceiling was a series of skylights with plants bursting from containers. The air was smooth, clean, and perfumed, the floor tiles polished to a mirror-like shine; by a water cooler stood a footman, ready to pour a drink.

In front of Verruca were two cleaners polishing a corner with bored expressions of repetition.

Cleaner One looked up and eyed Verruca.

"You after Herself?" said Cleaner One.

"How did you know?"

"She's the only one on the floor."

"But it's huge," said Verruca.

"Around the corner and to the right," said Cleaner Two, gesturing. "But mind, she's not in the best of moods."

"Too right, she been screaming like a banshee," said Cleaner One. "Best leave it for another day." She stopped. "Unless you've got batteries."

Hilda, dressed and ready for action in her Darth Vader cape and mask, opened the door; *time for "sorting" Verruca and whatever jumped-up, stupid gherkin idea she has.*

She peeked into the corridor. The cleaners had moved around the corner. *The coast is clear.*

With a muffled whistle, she called her floating platform, allowed it to slide under her feet, and, for the first time in days, headed into the passageway.

She thought about a plan . . . she had none. She didn't even know where Verruca was. *Is this what pelvic pleasure did to one? I'll wing it,* she told herself. *After all, Verruca is way past her sell-by date, probably using out-of-date spy tactics.* She laughed. *Like a blacked-out face.*

She decided to skirt down to the lobby incognito, checking any secret nooks and corners on the way. She was bound to bump into Verruca somewhere.

Verruca, looking like a poor man's Obi-Wan Kenobi, headed down the corridor. Clutching her stick like it was a lightsaber, Verruca thought about the past. She had fought in many battles, but that was years ago, before Hilda was even out of the shed.

She had one chance to catch Hilda off guard . . .

Her plan was to knock her out, slip the batteries into the drill, and then switch it on before Hilda woke up.

There were a few holes in the plan, mainly that she had no idea where the drill was or how the whole knocking-out-and-waking-up process should go.

She looked at Alice gesturing to the right. Verruca nodded. *Bet she'd know.*

Cleaner One turned off her hoover as Cleaner Two, leaning over the hoover transporter, stopped to watch.

Neither noticed Deidre appear until she tapped Cleaner One on the shoulder, causing both to start.

"Pickling polish, you nearly stopped my heart," she muttered.

"Just wondering what's going on." She eyed the back of Verruca. "I mean why is she creeping around like a Star Wars reject?"

"Shhhh," hissed Operator Two.

Verruca disappeared around the corner . . .

Chapter Thirty

PENCILS AND CRAYONS

"The lead in a pencil is only as good as the sharpener." –The H-Pad 11

The secretary rubbed her arm as Operator Three closed the door to a thud of pencils hitting it.

"That thing is evil," muttered the secretary.

The others nodded.

"Pure evil."

"Probably connected to Hilda," muttered a footman. "Saw her gulping like a blowfish—sure sign."

The secretary threw him an "and you said nothing" look.

"I thought she's on holiday," said Operator One.

"Well she won't be once that thing gets to her, will she? That . . . that pencil pusher has heard everything your H2 has said."

"She's not my H2."

"Who cares who said what—what are we to do next?" said Operator Four.

The screen, still in operational position on the table, began to play a "connections ready" fanfare.

"What is it now?" snapped Operator One. "This ruling lark really is the bollocks of all jobs."

DBO's face appeared on the screen. Behind her was Vegas and a band of women posed with unrecognizable instruments in a field.

The Operators stared at the LEADER splashed across DBO's chest, trying to work out why she was so familiar.

Who did they know with glasses?

"You need to find the receptor," said DBO.

The Operators looked at each other . . .

"In the room with a view?" said Operator Three.

DBO turned to Vegas, and Vegas nodded. "It's outside somewhere. You need to speak to the cook."

"We have just been penciled within an inch of our lives and you want us to face that again?" said the secretary. "I mean what has she got to do with energy, anyway?"

"She cooks with it," muttered a voice from the back.

"It is doable, I suppose," said Operator Two. "We could go the back way." She looked at Operator One with a "you and me" look.

Operator One glared at her with an "again" glare.

"And we have the footmen," said Operator Four.

The footmen jumped to attention.

"They could toss water as you leave."

DBO, peering from a set of plans, shouted, "It's behind the shed . . . well, it was."

The Operators stopped . . . and looked at the face behind the glasses.

"So that's who was missing," muttered someone.

Chapter Thirty-One

DARTH VADER

"No one tells me to feed my scones to the fish and gets away with it." —Kitchen wall (author unknown)

*D*eidre and the two cleaners stared at the corner.

Crash! Clutter!

"Bollocks!"

A pencil shot from the corner.

They raced to find Verruca using her stick to hold Hilda in a head-lock, Hilda gagging from the burnt tofu, and the H-Pad II firing pencils, crayons, and even the odd eraser like a tennis ball machine on speed.

A loud *thump* came from the door of the room with a view.

The Operators jumped.

The door crashed open and the cleaners raced into the room.

"Fight! Fight!"

Mex bristled. "Without me? Impossible."

DBO peered into the screen. "Fight? Who's fighting?"

"Some old lady with a smudged face and another in a cape—she came out of Hilda's pad," said Cleaner One.

"Like something out of Star Wars," added Cleaner Two.

"When we left they were heading for the speech balcony rolling about like . . . like . . ."

"Two mice over a lump of tofu," said Cleaner Two.

DBO looked about. "Coordinates for the speech balcony—anyone have them?

Vegas jumped. "Here."

A picture flashed on the screen. Verruca, having lost control, was now bent backward over the speech balcony, and Hilda, clutching Verruca's stick, was pressing it against her chest with a menacing if not downright mad look. Behind her were Alice and Deidre, vainly dodging flying pencils from the H-Pad 11.

Mex jumped into action. "I need but just one."

Silence.

She looked around and spotted H2's footman. "You'll do."

She turned to H2. "Set up those energy connections, I'll sort your gran."

Mex and H2's footman raced through the corridor, the footman puffing but doing his best.

They passed a water-cooler robot filling the cup dispenser with a footman feigning supervision.

"They went that-away," the footman shouted like a smart aleck.

Mex carried on at high speed.

H2's footman stopped to catch his breath.

"Water," muttered the smart aleck.

"Oh come on!" shouted Mex, disappearing around the corner. "No time for sipping."

Deidre grabbed the flying platform and tossed it to Verruca.

Verruca caught it in one hand.

The H-Pad 11 took aim—an eraser hit Verruca's eye.

The flying board fell from her hand and clattered to the floor.

Hilda tried to catch it; her fingers clipped the side.

Verruca kicked it.

Hilda made a lunge as it dropped over the ledge. "Nooooooo . . ."

Verruca took her chance and knocked Hilda to the ground, then jumped on top with a belly-flop move.

The H-Pad 11's pencils began to trickle out shorter, unsharpened bits of wood; producing erasers had taken up more energy than it realized. It was flagging.

Verruca and Hilda rolled across the floor, grunting and swearing.

Mex appeared with the footman while Alice slid away into Hilda's room with the batteries.

Hilda grabbed Verruca by the scruff of her collar and, in one lifting motion, rammed her to the wall.

Verruca, grabbing Hilda's scruff, pushed back . . . ramming her against the "ideas for speeches" board. Notes, pins, and pictures of Hilda cascaded to the floor.

Alice looked about Hilda's room. *Where is it?*

She searched the bedroom, the wardrobe, the drawers, the kitchen, the oven, the fridge, and finally, out of sheer desperation, the bin. There, dumped like a used tissue, on top of Verruca's "to the best leader," sat the drill.

It was not easy to lift out; amidst the shouts and grunts from the speech room, she dropped it several times. Alice heard a yell and looked up to see Verruca's stick shoot across the window, tofu splattered in its path. She started to panic. How much longer could Verruca last without her stick?

She must hurry . . .

She pulled the packet of batteries from her under-cage and looked at the "pull here" on the corner of the packet.

"Shit."

Hilda pushed Verruca back.

She, skidding on a "let's hear it for Hilda" poster, crashed onto the "put your feet up" recycled, whisper-thin, imitation-porcelain table.

"Not my porcelain," yelled Hilda as it shattered into pieces.

Verruca scrambled to her feet, grabbed the only intact table leg, and made a swing for Hilda.

"Won't be yours for long," she yelled.

Hilda ducked and the leg crashed against the wall.

Alice pulled, twisted, and tugged. Finally it hit her—*scissors*.

Mex pulled out her tiny whip and cracked it against a wall.

"Right, you lot—that's enough."

A stub of a pencil bounced off her shoulder and she turned to the H-Pad 11, now panting.

"Just sit over there, I will deal with you later."

An eraser oozed from a slit. Mex pushed it back in.

"I said sit!"

The H-Pad 11 slid into a corner.

Verruca backed Hilda into the beverage corner. Hilda scrambled for a cup and threw it at Verruca; deluxe soya milk splattered onto her face.

"Enough," shouted Mex with a second crack of her whip.

Hilda and Verruca glared at each other, panting . . .

"Deidre's here," said Mex.

"Who?"

"Me," said Deidre with a wave.

"Do you think she wants to see this sort of wrestling shenanigans?" Silence . . .

"From a so-called leader and . . ." She looked at Verruca's smudged face.

Verruca licked her lips.

"I mean what is she going to do, report the esteemed leader for fighting with a pencil pusher?"

Hilda looked at the floor. "She started it."

"She did," muttered Verruca.

"I did not . . ."

"You're the one done up like Darth Vader," snapped Verruca.

"That's because I have a face like mashed pumpkin. What's your excuse? Put your makeup on in the dark?"

Deidre unraveled a fountain tip from her hair, pulled her camera out, shouted "Smile!" to Hilda and Verruca, and clicked.

Hilda and Verruca blinked at the old-fashioned flash as the noise from Hilda's drill filled the corridor.

Hilda stopped and looked uncomfortable.

Verruca suppressed a smile.

"Perhaps Ma'am should rest for a bit while we sort out the energy crisis," said the footman, guiding her to her room.

"My porcelain," muttered Hilda.

"Maybe a foot rub to start with?" added the footman.

Chapter Thirty-Two

STRIP THE WILLOW

"It was a relief to retire from the whole procreating thing." –The Legless Odyssey

*I*n his youth, Legless had an animalistic presence—charisma, which as soon as he opened his mouth disappeared like the women he talked to. No one was interested in what he had to say, and it didn't take him long to use his body instead.

His hands were as soft as velvet and as strong as the grip on a jam jar—giving pleasure came as easy to him as peeling a banana. He could scan a body and read a mind like others read their lottery ticket. With just one look he could sweep a woman off her feet, and by the time she had removed her jacket, Legless knew everything—her needs, dreams, and fantasies, even what she liked in her coffee.

He always left a woman smiling—until his prostate kicked in.

Now, as he danced with the sixty-five-year-old nurse, he wondered how long it would be before she would want more than he could give.

The nurse's mind was a labyrinth of sorrow and good works. Her life, despite helping others, had been lonely . . . and her sadness touched him.

It's been so long since I've laughed, she thought, *I can't remember what it was about.*

He twirled her around.

*Make me laugh—*she looked at him—*like her over there.*

Legless shouted to the band to turn it up and give this "Jacobean lassie something to remember—Jimmy Shand style."

DJ, unsure what Jacobean had to do with dancing, pulled out his spoons and nodded to the band. "A polka."

The song started with a crisp drumroll, and as the accordion twinkled into action, Don gave Gary a "what for" about his "outrageous pulling up."

"Get your fiddle out," he snapped.

Gary pulled a "must I" face, but he didn't have a leg to stand on. Every Identity played an instrument; it was not only part of the initiation but used to control behavior such as Gary's. In fact, Gary's bad behavior was so frequent that he was more on the stage than off, his fiddling as legendary as his ability to pull up when not asked.

As Gary lifted his fiddle, Legless and the nurse twirled, skipped, and circled faster and faster until her hair tumbled from her bun. It was fun, but not what she was looking for . . .

She was looking for the perfect dance, the dance she did years ago, back in the good ol' days of wards and young med students, and she would not rest till she found it.

Other women watched with distaste; they were fed up with her. The nurse not only hogged the floor but nudged a "swap" with everyone's partners just as the going was good.

"Totally abusing the nudging law," said some.

The nurse didn't care. She firmly believed in the right to nudge and swap and no one was going to stop her.

The women had had enough. "Give us a 'Strip the Willow'?" shouted a blonde. "Let's see her nudge her way out of that."

"Yeah!" shouted another. *Anything to get that show off of the floor . . .*

Don and Bunnie watched the couples lined up, Identities on one side and women on the other.

"Why don't we sit this one out and wait for something slower?" he said. Bunnie didn't argue.

Beryl, standing at the end of the line waited her turn. The first couple began, a twirl and a yell—*I could do that.* She waited, clapping like the others, giving it her all, when her turn came. She swirled Ed like a hammer throw, his kilt ruffled high above his athletic hips. The nurse caught a glimpse and smiled.

I want him.

Legless and the nurse were next; they moved down the line, twirling each person they met. The nurse, hell-bent on making it to Ed, skirted through the other partners in double time. Legless, feeling a little seasick, tried to keep up, and by the time he got to Beryl, he was puffed, his kilt askew like laundry caught in the wind.

He caught her eye.

Beryl smiled, he didn't . . .

They twirled.

You still here? he ESP-ed.

Yes.

No one left to double-cross then?

Well, no.

Beryl moved back to the line as Legless danced on.

There must have been a better way of saving the planet . . . Legless glared.

There were budgets. Beryl blushed with shame.

After three rounds of "Strip the Willow," the music stopped. The nurse had out-twirled everyone, leaving those in her path puffed and panting. As Legless stopped for a breather, she made her claim for the young and virile Ed.

She turned to Beryl.

"Swap," she snapped.

"What?"

"I said swap."

Beryl bristled. "Don't you tell me to *swap*."

Ed shifted uncomfortably. "Swapping is part of the protocol."

Beryl blinked at him.

"When one says swap, you must do so," said the blonde with a tired voice.

The nurse, with an "exactly," nudged Beryl out of the way, grabbed Ed, and dragged him like a child onto the floor.

"Can we not wait for the music?" he muttered.

She threw back her head and laughed. He was all hers for the taking.

Chapter Thirty-Three

THE REKINDLING OF THINGS

"Good riding requires more than a decent bike." —Legless's Blue Period

Don took Bunnie downstairs to the empty café.

Bunnie was trying to come to terms with Legless. He was her Johnny, the best escort she ever had, so hard to believe in the flesh. He looked nothing like the man she imagined, who had kept women happy for years until, as he put it, the prostate kicked in.

Don slid a hot chocolate across to Bunnie.

"Hard to believe they are the same," she muttered. "Explains the terrible writing."

"Archie says the same," said Don. "Called him a dickhead."

Bunnie laughed. "What do you think?"

Don expanded on his "Beryl's the missing link" theory. "You never know, there may be a good story in him yet."

"Hmmm," said Bunnie with a bored look.

Don nudged her. "You know how you're talking of painting your bedroom?"

"I never said anything about paint—"

"Why not let me do it?"

She turned and looked at him. "You in my bedroom?" She laughed. "Do you have a big enough brush?"

"Brush?" said Don. "Mine is the size of a roller."

Bunnie chuckled. "Aye, but can it get into all the nooks and crannies?"

"Nooks? I am an expert at them."

Don looked into Bunnie's eyes. Her face softened. Neither heard the talk upstairs or the cars outside; instead, they gazed like they had never really seen each other before.

"Funny place, this," muttered Bunnie.

Don touched her lips. "You're anything but funny."

"And you, Mr Don, are a—" She stopped as Don kissed her just long enough for her to want more.

Beryl looked at the aged face of Legless. He met her stare with a gasp; after all these years, she still did that to him.

"You're looking good for your age," she lied.

"I look like an old man," said Legless. "And it's all because of you."

"Me?"

"Yes, you. You treated me like a piece of meat."

"Meat? I never touch the stuff."

"I was just a cyclist to you, wasn't I?"

Silence.

"A Lycra-wearing, energy-making slave. You didn't care about me at all, did you?"

No reply.

"There is more to me and you know it."

Beryl blushed.

"Why else would you send me here to . . . impregnate?"

She stopped. "Impregnate? Did I say anything about impregnating?"

"You didn't have to, it's all over the place here. It's a given."

"Since when is that sort of thing a given?"

"Don't lie, you knew it would happen. Everyone knows about Earth women."

The music stopped.

"You fertilized more eggs than our fertilizing lab; did you have to be so prolific?"

"It was on a plate!" yelled Legless.

The room was silent apart from the nurse cackling with Ed in the corner. Everyone glared at Legless.

". . . not that you cared."

"I am hardly a plate to dip in," muttered a voice from the back.

"How do you think that made me feel?" muttered Beryl.

"Feel? You? When have you ever felt anything?" said Legless. "Unlike you, these women appreciated the effort. I made them happy."

"Five minutes under a clothesline is hardly foreplay," muttered an Identity.

Foreplay? thought Beryl.

Legless shot a look at the Identity. "We all have to start somewhere. You try shagging on another planet, see how long it takes you to get the hang of it."

Legless huffed. He looked about at the Identities.

"It's not easy, jumping into a new world looking like you know what you're doing."

"You hardly jumped," muttered Beryl.

"See, that's what I mean. Your Earth words—they're all mixed up."

He stopped.

"Look, I know I'm not exactly a legend."

They looked unimpressed.

"But this place is confusing. The chewing gum on the streets, but spitting is frowned on."

"Except if you're a footballer," muttered an Identity.

"You call animals names and then eat them, and what the hell does 'well done' mean? Burnt to a crisp, job done better than expected; well done, knob head?"

"Why don't you go back then?" shouted the blonde.

"Ask her." Legless gestured to Beryl.

Beryl squirmed. "It's a long story."

"Long story? You did the dirty on me, there is nothing long about that," he huffed. "I lived in a cave because of you."

The identities stopped. *You lived in a cave?*

Legless shuffled. "Sometimes, well, now and then." He looked at the blank faces. "The odd day . . . it's good for thinking."

What the hell's a cave? thought Beryl.

Legless looked about the unconvinced faces. *This is not going to plan . . .*

"I could have been a leader on that planet," he stammered.

The Identities, looking at Legless in disbelief, began to answer back . . .

"You were a leader here until you went to your so-called cave."

"Left us for dead."

"And a mess."

"My mum cried for weeks."

"Mine stopped shaving her legs."

"It's women who lead where I come from," said Beryl.

"Yes, and look at the mess that made," said Legless.

"Women lead here too," said a woman from the back.

Beryl said nothing.

"That spark plug was my idea," muttered Legless.

"Spark plug? Who the hell uses them?" said Gary, who was also a mechanic of sorts.

Legless tried to explain, but as the others laughed, he withdrew.

DJ said nothing. Somehow, watching the demise of his father wasn't as great as he expected.

"You're a laughingstock," said Gary. "I can't believe I wanted to meet you. I was so excited today when you connected, and now you're talking of spark plugs?"

The identities nodded in agreement. *Hear, hear . . .*

Gary continued, "What's next, a steering column gear? Phone boxes? I mean look at you. You're just an old git who could do with a decent shave."

Silence . . .

"You took that too far," muttered someone.

Legless slumped into a seat and his kilt flopped between his legs like an old tea towel. *What a stupid idea it was—me coming here.*

DJ told Gary to shut it.

Gary told DJ to shut it and added a few abusive gestures with his fiddle.

Archie told Gary to treat his fiddle with more respect.

Gary, working up to more insults, rammed his fiddle into its case and was about to say something involving a fair amount of swearing when Beryl jumped in.

"Where I come from, a spark plug is an innovation," she said.

"Pfff," said Gary.

"And old people are honored with statues."

"They do that here," muttered the blonde.

Beryl looked at Legless, vulnerable and broken. "And this shell of a man here—"

"Steady on," muttered Legless.

"—will be the next statue."

A few gasped . . .

Legless sat up. *Seriously?*

"He saved our planet."

Silence.

"You are standing in the presence of a hero," said Beryl, who, used to making speeches to an unresponsive crowd, launched into a speech that told the story of Legless, leaving little except any unheroic bits.

"Give him another chance," she finished, "like I hope he does me,"

A few clapped.

Beryl sat beside him and, for the first time in her life, put her arms around another.

"I'm sorry," she said.

More cheered.

"Now that's what I call an apology," said Archie.

Chapter Thirty-Four

A NEW MARKET

"When I think of my mum, I hold my stomach in, pull back my shoulders, and curse my lousy bra. Mum always tied high." – Bunnie

few months later

H2 skulled her coffee and poured another, then picked up her H-Pad to clean. Communication between the Operators, the hippie colony, and the fieldworkers was not always easy, and it was her who had to smooth things. Cleaning helped her plan.

"Foot rub?" said her footman, posing with a bottle of oil.

"Not now, but you can get me Alice," she said.

"Consider it done, ma'am."

Alice was with DBO at the market. DBO, along with Vegas, had transformed the market into a place sheltered from rain, and bartering was frown upon. It was a place open to anyone to buy or sell. Even the Voted In had a stall for their paintings; what else could they do in the basement now that their cycling was no longer needed?

DBO walked the market. There were issues with the sell-by dates which she needed to nip in the bud before Deidre got wind.

She picked up a jar, looked at the date, and sniffed. "Put it at half price and we'll say no more."

The stall worker nodded as DBO moved on.

"Half price implemented," she said to Alice.

"Affirmative," said Vegas.

"Excellent," said H2.

DBO moved on to the "tofu that tastes like sausage" stall and made an "anyone remember what a *real* sausage tastes like" joke. Some laughed, others offered her a gift. DBO refused all.

"Here, have a wrap," said a stall owner.

"Lovely," said DBO as she made to pay.

The stall worker shook her head, but DBO placed the money on the bench, implementing the new "pay for everything" policy. H2 had promised a "no backhanders" regime, which for the most part was obeyed.

"How long will that last?" muttered the stall owner.

Hilda waited until Vegas was out of earshot and shouted, "Give her time."

No one heard. The band was situated next to her stall, and no matter how many times she shouted, they kept playing. The band, now with a full set of proper drums and real string instruments, pulled out all the stops when Hilda was about, and when she wasn't, they paused, often laughing about the good old days when they played tunes on kitchen equipment.

Hilda was seen as a traitor, and thanks to Deidre, she had fallen.

Deidre's "the real price for leaders" column had forced Hilda out of power and into the workforce—selling vibrators in the stall under the management of Verruca—and every day, Hilda faced the silent treatment. Not that it bothered her; she had plans to wear them down. She watched all the time, determined to make a success and debunk the whole *there are only so many ways you can flog a vibrator* theory, which many threw at her on a daily basis.

She wrote reviews and articles on the different prototypes, always in a onesie; she claimed it kept her mind sharp, which had Verruca's robot doubling over with laughter. Hilda, with nowhere else to go, had moved in with Verruca, whose house was now improved with a garden worth sitting in. Hilda and the robot moaned about Verruca behind her back and spent their time setting up the screen on the fridge to collapse as soon as she switched it on. And despite the discomfort of a damp bed, Hilda had never laughed so much.

Pete still lived with Mex. They, along with Woody, were an integral part of the new scaled-down room with a view. The Operators welcomed Woody and Pete but were still adjusting to Mex, despite her tossing her whip aside.

To win them over, Mex often resorted to tales of Earth, which, once Woody joined in, had them chuckling in their now-free-for-the-masses coffee.

Pete loved to regale them with talk of ferries, the roll-off-and-on method of cars, and sea sickness, with a gentle nod at Mex.

"Throwing up is an experience you'd never want," said Pete with an effeminate gesture of a napkin, "although Bunnie's brandy made it almost worth it."

"Brandy, how droll," laughed some.

"That would turn even a robot into a crooner."

"Crooner, how *very* droll."

The Operators couldn't get enough of the stories, often telling Pete to "write them down," with an extended chapter on Earth finger gestures.

"Giving the finger" had the Operators in stitches.

Beryl moved into sheltered accommodation near Legless. It was Archie's idea. And while Beryl got used to ferry crossings and visits from Bunnie, Legless took it upon himself to acclimatize his ex-master to the wonders of Scotland and beyond. So far, they had visited every museum in the area, had numerous picnics at the planetarium, and been to three coffee mornings, unsure if it was their thing or not.

They also spent a great deal of time in his shed, sorting his hens, and on a good day, Beryl stayed over—on the couch. Legless, however, was working a getting-Beryl-off-the-couch-and-into-his-bedroom ploy. He, taking a page out of Don's book, had sorted his bedroom, and Beryl, inspired by IKEA, sometimes helped . . .

Beryl, despite everyone staring at her beehive, still sprayed it every day and even found a hairdresser who just "loved the whole concept." Beryl introduced Legless to the hairdressers, who not only gave his look a revamp but told him about pelvic exercises.

"It's all in the squeezing, man," he said. "Honestly, I thought I could never manage a long journey again, and look at me—dribble free and loving it."

Beryl still kept in contact with Mex and, hearing the latest on Hilda, decided for the moment that visiting museums with Legless were way better than working at a market stall, especially now that the band had new instruments. Besides, she had grown to like pushing a co-op trolley with Legless. His explanation of "buy one get one free" had her, to quote him, "pissing herself," and as for the "crack" with a checkout attendant, it was almost as good as a foot rub.

EPILOGUE

Archie and DJ were organizing a meeting for the weekend. It was to be held in the Storytelling Center during the World Storytelling Festival. Identities were coming from as far as Canada, Australia, and even Mongolia. Legless was top billing; thanks to Beryl's management, his stories had become something of a legend.

Archie and DJ parked their car in a spot that Don knew about. "I know friends in high places and low," he said, "and many who would give a bed for the night and more."

Bunnie laughed. "Well, that's not happening, now is it."

Bunnie had given up her business of matchmaking; with Don resident in her newly painted bedroom, pairing people up had lost its attraction. Instead, they ran a bed-and-breakfast and took turns frying the bacon, arguing about how crisp it should be.

Eunice was a bit miffed. She had managed to create many stories from Bunnie's business, a bed-and-breakfast was hardly inspiring. But there were new things on the horizon.

Mex had remained connected—she wanted videos of Izzie, and Patsy (bless her) was negotiating.

There could be a new series of stories about a planet run by women with a heroine who had a thing for dogs . . . you never know.

❄

Beryl walked into the museum with Legless; they were heading for the planetarium next door. Every week, they visited museums. Beryl loved them, and Legless, finally finding a way to please that didn't involve "prostate issues," was happy to oblige.

Beryl entered the first room of the "women through the ages" exhibition, which always had her confused.

She listened to the voiceover, mouthing the words . . .

"In the beginning, culture, art, and music came together, creating myths of long-forgotten planets illustrating the conquest of conquering."

She stared at the first cabinet full of pottery figures—round terracotta women proudly showing their breasts, some clutching instruments—and not for the first time wondered, *Are they talking of my planet?*

". . . evidence of habitation of women goddesses."

Beryl peered at their sculptured faces with indented eye features that became evident in the shadow of the light. Legless pushed her on, impatient for the laughter.

She stopped at the next cabinet, full of thin veiled women of painted clay . . .

"Come on," muttered Legless. "You've seen this before."

"Women portrayed as helpless, chained, and sold . . ."

"Chained," she muttered, confused, "and sold?"

Legless ushered her though the door. "Keep moving . . . nearly there."

Beryl looked up at the "comic book heroes" scrawled at the top of the doorway and smiled. Now this room is funny . . .

She laughed "Captain America, Batman, Superman, Wolverine. If only they could see these bozos on Planet Hy Man."

Later that day, as Legless bent over the fire, grunting a joke she couldn't quite hear, Beryl put her feet up and sighed. She never tired of looking at his back side and as the flames flickered casting shadows across his builder's crack, she realized that sleeping on the couch was no longer what she really wanted.

Would you like to read more? The back story of your favourite characters?
Rebel Without A Mask Book 4 is out now at your favourite store.
If you would like a sneak preview then please keep reading.

REBEL WITHOUT A MASK

Chapter One-For The Love Of Beryl

"One woman's orgasm is another's 'It was OK.'"—Legless after a few whiskies

Legless looked at Beryl: still and cool. She was breathing deeply but silent.

After making love, Beryl had dropped off quicker than a belch, hardly moving from her back—not a snore, a sniff, or even a mutter.

Years of maintaining a beehive hairdo can do that to a woman. Well, that and a childhood spent sleeping in a cabin bed the size of a small trunk.

Beryl always fell asleep before Legless, but tonight was different. They had made love, and now he was watching her.

It had been a long time.

He stared at the stars from their window.

No matter how many planetariums they had been to, he was still confused; he had no idea what stars were which. Sometimes he thought he recognized something, perhaps the Milky Way. He knew Planet Hy Man was somewhere in the same region; he had heard Beryl talk of it.

There were times he had looked at the stars and yearned for home, to go back, wreak havoc on Beryl and her Voted In's, cause a downfall, and have her at her knees.

But not now.

Tonight he looked at the stars through the exhausted eyes of a man after a satisfying shag. It had been a while, and despite Beryl's lack of interest, he had pulled it off, turned her on, pleased her like the good old days when they first "hooked up" on Earth.

He made his way downstairs, heated up yesterday's coffee, and, sipping with an "arrrrh," pulled out his writing implement.

He typed: "The Conquest of Beryl."

This will have them on the edge of their seat. He smiled. *They'll have to let me make a speech now . . .*

When they'd first slept together on Planet Hy Man, Legless had dropped off quicker than a nose dribble, his smooth face as peaceful as a monk.

Legless had taken Beryl by surprise; after a lusty eye exchange and a quick fumble, Legless led her to a cupboard of a room.

"Let's see what we have here," he whispered.

And before she had time to answer, her leathers were off, her corset untied and erect on the floor, and Beryl was gasping on a trolley the size of her childhood cabin bed.

He was a young man enjoying the luscious effects of Planet Hy Man's atmosphere. His nose was a silent hair-free breathing apparatus, while his bladder was strong, capable of holding a keg of beer without a dribble. And as for his apparatus, it was as efficient as a fire hose, quenching pent-up passion that took them both by surprise.

As Beryl's back arched in pleasure, he moaned, sighed, then rolled off, asleep before he hit the floor. Landing on a pile of laundry, he didn't feel a thing, let alone wake up, unaware that he had the legendarily coldhearted Beryl crying with laughter . . .

Years later, when Legless took Beryl for the first time on Earth, it was more a fumble, the eye exchange more wistful than lusty.

There was no comedy fall, more a delicious sigh as they lay, spread-eagled, with surprise. Neither had any idea that their body could pull off past antics with such precision.

Afterward, a sweaty and still-a-little-stunned Legless headed into the kitchen.

"Fancy a cuppa?" he yelled.

"OK," she yelled back with no idea what a cuppa was.

She slid under the sheets and almost giggled.

It had taken a few months for Legless to "conquer," as he liked to call it, despite Beryl visiting almost daily.

The sheltered accommodation Archie had arranged was not exactly what Beryl was looking for. She found the constant wandering of inmates a tad disturbing, the warden's early morning call as inspiring as the mobile hairdresser trying to talk Beryl into a "less dated" look.

She preferred Legless's home, and once she learned to drive, she was never out of the place, despite the mess, derelict cars, and broken hen house. She couldn't stay away.

Beryl had taken to driving like a child to McDonald's.

It had been a year since Beryl and Legless met in Edinburgh. A year since Bunnie, with a toot of her horn, picked Beryl and Legless up from the B&B, since Beryl first pressed the accelerator of a car . . .

Bunnie had been driving Beryl and Legless to their new home in Dunoon when a foot cramp struck like a sledgehammer.

Bunnie, mid steering, let out a shriek, and Beryl, without thinking, grabbed the wheel.

Her ability to maneuver Bunnie's four-wheel onto the Dunoon ferry surprised not only Bunnie but Beryl herself. She had only driven once—on Planet Hy Man—and she'd been so young she could hardly touch the peddles.

Legless, dozing in the back, jumped to attention, and before he could get a word in about gears, she was changing them, sliding Bunnie's four-wheel drive into a parking space like a seasoned taxi driver.

A year on, Beryl still jumped behind the wheel excited as a teenager in a porn shop.

She loved cars; she loved driving, especially to Legless's home and his animals—or his "menagerie," as he liked to call it.

She loved to stroke "Sophia," his scraggy cat, toss leftovers to his moth-eaten dog, Bark Twain, their earthy smells mesmerizing her until she let them inside.

Feeding his hens—or "the girls," as he liked to call them—fascinated her as much as their names: Gina, Lollo, Bridget, and Bardo. She could spend hours watching them, not to mention Charlton Heston the cockle with a strut so majestic even Bark Twain stopped to watch.

But what she loved most was to watch Legless light his fire for her to sleep by on the couch.

He had a nice back, apart from his thin ponytail trailing down it.

She never said anything, but Legless read her mind, and one day the ponytail was gone and Legless was feeling hopeful.

Beryl arrived to find Legless bent over the hearth, cleaning with a grunt.

He lit his standard minuscule fire lighter and waited for the flames to take hold.

The flames flickered, illuminating his perfect round skull. She stopped.

"Shall I get the blankets?" he said without turning around.

"Not tonight," she said.

He looked at her with a grin.

"Let's give that IKEA bed of yours a go," she whispered.

Bark Twain poked his head around the corner, took one look at Legless's naked rump straddled across Beryl, and made for the kitchen, his cushion, and a bowl of water.

Umpteen moans later, Beryl looked out from his IKEA bed with the sort of smile she hadn't cracked since Legless left Planet Hy Man. The sort of smile that would have the Voted Ins and Bunnie choking on their caffeine.

It was a smile that lit up her face; she glowed.

She had really missed Legless: the smell of his warm body, his ability to not only push the right button but do it for the best length of time . . . a knack not even human men knew of.

A couple of minutes under Legless's hands and she was back in that cupboard of a room getting to know her private bits like never before.

She slid further under the sheets, peering at the bedroom they had decorated together as Legless entered the room dribbling tea from two mugs.

She eyed his thin legs poking from his baggy boxers and started to laugh.

"No pickling milk," he muttered.

"Milk? That stuff from cows?" She pulled a face. "I heard it makes men grow breasts."

He looked at her, stuck out his flat chest, and laughed. "Like these?" he said.

She stared at his sprinkling of grey hairs and sighed.

He handed her a mug; she sipped, pulled a face.

"No caffeine?" she said.

"Not what you like," he muttered. "Packet stuff, way worse than that." He gestured to her mug.

She sipped again. The taste grew on her. A bit bitter, but . . . she gulped another mouthful, swallowed it down . . . it warmed her.

"I could get used to this," she finally said.

Soon he had a cupboard full and was trying teas like a true tea jenny. And each time Legless pleasured her, it was he who opened the cupboard and stared at the growing number of packets, shouting . . .

"Herbal? Earl Grey? What is Ma'am's pleasure today?"

On sale at your favourite store.

A NOTE FROM THE AUTHOR

I hope you enjoyed adventures of Pete, Woody and all the crew.
I love men in kilts and I love story telling.
Over the years I have told many stories, some to a paid audience...but
never have I worn a kilt.
Apart from a prickly affair as child, it was more a skirt that was too hot
in summer and kept little warm in winter.
And I was way too young for a sporran!

You can find me and my groovy blogs at
www.kerrienoor.com
And

 facebook.com/planetHyman

 x.com/kezzamac

 instagram.com/kerrienoor

OTHER BOOKS BY KERRIE A NOOR

Planet Hy Man Series
Book 1:- Rebel Without A Clue
Book 2: Rebel Without A Bra
Book 3 Rebel Without A Crew
Prequels
Prequel 1 The Rise Of Manifesto The Great
Prequel 2 The Downfall Of Manifesto The Great
Prequel 3 The Legacy Of Manifesto The Great

And Finally
If you love **Rebel without a Crew**. I would really appreciate a short
review., in fact my gratitude would hold no bounds.
Regards and Cheers
Kerrie A Noor